ALL THE LOVE IN THE WORLD

A Premiered Collection of Adults Stories to Enjoy Your Lockdown Time

Rose Reed

Table of Contents

13 stories: 13 Premiered Age-Proof Sex Stories

14 stories: The JIXX Book of Hidden Pleasure

15 stories: BROKEN IN!

13 stories: 13 Premiered Age-Proof Sex Stories

Sex Stories

The Hottest Erotic Collection of 2021 at Your Fingertips!

Rose Reed

Table of Contents

THE CELEBRATION

Eighty-six thousand, six hundred and twenty-one dollars.

The end result is equal to the money we raised that night. We had driven through the county and north across the state border, collecting green garbage bags with the bills locked up in self-storage facilities. The sacks were usually wrapped in an old, tattered paint sheet or hidden between similar sacks filled with used clothing of scrap dealer quality. The collected sacks filled both trunks of large American cars when it was over.

We had taken two vehicles with us - one following the other close enough to offer protection, but far enough away not to be detected. I drove with my friend Ronnie. He was the only one who knew where we were going until we got there. Both cars were equipped with handguns for each man and also a sawn-off shotgun for each man in the back seat - one in each car. It was the first time I had seen Ronnie or any of his guys with loaded guns.

It was so scary I almost peed my pants, but I wanted to be more a part of Ronnie's world, and Ronnie's world was dangerous and illegal. It was a surreal experience from start to finish. That special kick you get when you know you shouldn't do something but feel so cool that you wouldn't miss it for the world.

I didn't know whether the weapons were to protect us from a possible robbery by rival groups or from a shoot-out in case of a police intervention. I didn't want to think about what could have happened either way.

Eighty-five thousand is probably not a lot of money by today's standards, but back then it was enough to buy a very nice house even in big cities. It was more money that I thought I would ever see in one go.

That was real drug money. It was not like in the movies with crisp hundred-dollar bills nicely stacked in a leather briefcase. The bills were wrinkled and torn from the time spent in blue jeans bags - enough to get a horny boy and his girlfriend high on Friday night. A teenager was given $5 to go to the roller rink, instead they were spent to buy a few loose joints. $20 that a fast-food worker made and used to buy a gram of crank. The change from a couple of trips to the store for the mother never returned to her and instead bought some black beauties.

These were street drug money, collected over time by some of Ronnie's local distributors. It was a bunch of it. Not a single $50 bill in the stack and very few of them. It was currently lying on my bedroom floor, stacked in stacks of $100 so we could count it all.

Ronnie and I had counted and recounted the money for hours - we stopped at regular intervals to laugh, drink, draw a line and fuck occasionally. It's a pretty hackneyed scene from a B-movie these days to see a drug dealer and his girlfriend rolling around on a bed of money, but we did it loud and proud, as if we'd invented the idea. Ronnie was pretty high from his nightly score, I could see that, and he rode me pretty hard, which I had no complaints about. The sex was electrifying and fun and became more and more inventive the further we went.

It was damn hot, and I enjoyed it so much that I couldn't think straight, and I let him throw me around on the bed so he could take me the way he wanted. I wanted him to take me and make me cum all over the money, even though some of the bills smelled pretty disgusting.

I was just a little uncomfortable because I knew that four of Ronnie's friends were in the house - all wired, buzzing and armed to the teeth. The creaking bed and the unsuppressed moans and giggles were nothing they hadn't heard before, but I tried not to think about it. (It's hard to have too much privacy when you live with a drug dealer).

Every time we finished fooling around, we had to count the stacks that we hadn't tied with rubber bands yet. I sat there naked and counted some of the money, which was maybe the third time, while Ronnie admired the view. Every now and then he'd break another piece of coke or roll up another joint, and if I was embarrassed, I'd beg him to stop.

After a while Ronnie realized that it had been a while since he had looked after his boys - and with over $80,000 in the house I could tell we were a bit paranoid, even though we were having a good time. He put his pants back on and left the bedroom to check in.

I heard them talking - and again reminded myself that they could hear us too - and heard one of the boys ask Ronnie "when it was their turn". It was Mark, a big bully of a man who had been driving all night with a shotgun in the back seat of the second car.

There was no humor in his voice. That wasn't Mark just bullying Ronnie. Suddenly everyone became calm, and even from the other room I felt a certain tension. It was a problem every time a bunch of drugged up gangsters got into an argument, but for me it was twice as important, because Ronnie was the only one in the bunch who wasn't heavily armed.

After a much too long silence, Ronnie murmured: "Dude, you haven't been here long, so I'm going to excuse you this time. She is different and she is mine... "You want some pussy, we'll get you some, but let's put the fucking booty away first."

I could tell by the footsteps that Ronnie had walked away from the door after he said this - his attempt to move the conversation away from the bedroom door and my ears. Mark didn't seem happy with the answer. He muttered, "It doesn't seem right - you're having all the fun while we're sitting out here with our tails in our hands. As time went by I would find this man more and more unpleasant.

When Ronnie came back into the room, he had a couple of big old suitcases with hard side walls in which we had piled $70,000 of the money. $5,000 he stuck to the bottom of drawers he'd taken out of my bedroom dresser and nightstand. Another $8,000 he sat aside to pay the boys - he slipped this into a brown lunch bag and dropped it next to the door.

Then he turned off the light and I suspected that this meant it was time for sleep, which was a good thing, since it was perhaps 4:00 in the morning. But Ronnie wasn't finished yet, and as soon as he was lying naked in bed he manoeuvred my head down and I knew exactly what he wanted me to do. While I was serving him, he gave me instructions - Ronnie never did that before. I knew he was mocking Mark.

That kind of theatricality was just part of living with Ronnie, and I had learned to find the humor and even the power in it. But this time I became restless and I tried to withdraw and tell him to stop. He had none.

He had his hands firmly on the back of my head and I could not stop until he had finished. Ronnie almost never came in my mouth, even when I wanted him to, so I knew that this was 100% for show. He knew that Mark was probably sitting outside the door. That was Ronnie - he let people know who was in charge. I could say that it made me feel cheap - but the truth is I kind of liked the feeling that I was special enough to cause friction.

When he finished, we finally fell asleep, but around 8:30 he woke me up to give me some instructions, saying he had to go away for a while.

He told me to take his $5,000 out of the dresser over the next few days, $500 each in 10 different checking accounts we had set up around the country. Ronnie also let me know that the $621 that wasn't in the thousands piles was mine.

I knew that the other guys had been promised $2000 each for night work - but I didn't feel cheated at all. I was just a feast for the eyes - not an armed bodyguard - and would probably have gone for nothing.

Finally he told me to put my hair up, put on some make-up, then put on the nightgown behind the door and make breakfast for the boys. He and I both knew that wearing this thing was so thin that it was almost like being naked, and that was the point.

I never met Ronnie at moments like this. I did what I was told - I understood my hair and my morning swollen face as best I could. I bent over to put on some panties, but Ronnie stopped me, shoved my ass and basically threw me out of the room.

The moment I hit the hallway, four pairs of eyes were hit by the body and remained there. The gown hung on me like wet paint, and I was painfully aware of this. Although all the shades in the house were closed because we were not afraid of prying eyes, enough sunlight still came in so that they could capture my silhouette through the thin fabric.

I continued to make breakfast, flinching inside whenever I had to bend down to get a pan or open the refrigerator with its bright interior light. Ronnie was right behind me on the way out of the bedroom, so at least I knew everyone would behave - and they did -

and thanked me for breakfast and even picked up their pies and put them in the sink when they were done - which they certainly didn't do at home.

Breakfast was served, Ronnie and the crew quickly packed up, and I didn't see or hear from them for almost a week. (I was worried all the time, too - I didn't even trust Ronnie's people when I knew there was $70,000 available there that they could consider their own and make with a few shots).

When I did, it was as if our lives suddenly shifted into a whole new gear. That $70,000 was used to buy us into a whole new business with higher stakes and higher payouts. I didn't know it at the time, but Ronnie had bought an area and sold his soul to a so-called cartel. They were less violent back then, but they were still people you don't know that well.

Before it was over, I would get too involved in all this, but I was young, naive, and all I knew was that we seemed ten feet tall and bulletproof. We had money, powder and power.

Until we didn't have it anymore.

THE LINE

It results from "should not" and "must not". "I can't, I don't want to". Please don't do this to me. It's a lie because every muscle in my body wants to touch me and my skin is burning to taste.

I'm going to say that he's my opposite and everything I shouldn't want and can't have. I can stand in front of him and just the sight of him makes the blood rush through me and make me throbbing. And I have no fucking idea why. But I do, of course I do. He's rough and stocky, and if I met him, I'd bounce off him. He's curvy and he's heavy and everything about him is bigger and stronger and uglier. He's my opposite, and I want him to defile my femininity. But he must not. I won't let him, because I belong with my husband.

But what if I were to...?

What if I didn't look away when I feel his eyes moving over my body? What if I leaned over the desk and allowed him a closer look at the cleavage, which I know he has spent many nights thinking about fucking. What if I whispered into his ear all the dirty things he does to me at night when I think about him.

It would be so easy to touch his chest while I do it that he would wonder if I had lost my mind or if he had finally broken my resolve. I wouldn't tell too soon - I would play flirtatiously, whisper a little "No, I can't" as he went in to kiss me.

He'd run his lips over mine as I pulled away. I can smell him; the oil of the machines he works with, the tingling of the new sweat, his breath and his body. I want the smell of him to stick to me as if he was marking me. He can see the conflict in my eyes.

I can't. I must not. But haven't I crossed the line already? Our lips met, so if I'm doomed to guilt, I should eat my fill.

In a split second of weakness, I press my lips to his. I feel the roughness of his beard, and his tongue feels strange as it enters my mouth. I am not used to being kissed like that by anyone else. I shouldn't do that. But as I cross that line, I realize again that I'm already ruined. All I can think about is the feeling of his big, rough fingers inside me.

I love that, and I'll tell him that. Nothing can save me now, because he hastily slides his hand under my skirt and I open my legs to give him access, as if I give in to his will or resign myself to it. My thoughts stray to the fact that we could be caught and there would be no covering up. Here I am, legs spread, sitting on his lap while he pushes my soaked underwear aside and the tips of his rough thick fingers probe the pink creases of my cunt. I feel ambushed as he sinks his fingers inside me, as if he is taking my second virginity. My innocence is gone; I am a fraud. It is beyond ecstasy. He knows what he is doing while waggling his fingers inside me. The pressure on my G-spot makes me squirm and whimper like a frightened animal out of control. I have spent so many nights thinking about this.

I see that his face is consumed with lust and I realize that although he is honestly excited to finger fuck me, I really want to give something back. His cock is hard through his pants, and if there is one thing I have thought about more than him finger-fucking me, it is the thought of blowing him. On my knees at his whim; the ultimate submission.

I already know he loves that. I figured it out from the subtle things he said and the way he looked at my lips. I remember once, at his request, I guiltily sent him a photo of my face. His joy at such an inexplicable image made me think...

So I kneel down, unzip and reveal the cock I had imagined for as long as I could stretch out every fuckhole I could offer. I want to show him what I can do. I spent years honing that skill on my husband. His cock is humble, and I'm grateful for that because it's easier to handle. I start with his balls, enjoy the taste he has and that unmistakable masculine smell. I like to lick and suck gently while giving a show of myself, making occasional eye contact with him. The insolence of my eye contact underlines my fall from grace. I want to be his bitch.

I lick and kiss the veins of his shaft. I look at the head of his cock glistening before coming. I like to play with him as if he were a lipstick by pulling the tip of his cock over my open lips. I can taste him. It is salty and warm and I enjoy it as if it were a delicacy. I know he's watching me, so I make sure he sees me willingly humiliating myself and my morals.

I suck gently at the tip, using mainly my lips and guiding it with my hand in my mouth. He's getting more and more urgent, so I allow him to fuck my mouth. The feeling he has in my mouth is satisfyingly uncomfortable. It's almost a sadomasochistic kick that I get. The elation brings my mind to bliss. I'm wet and throbbing between my legs. I want him to lick and fuck me until orgasm, but when his dick head presses into the back of my throat, it brings my orgasm mentally closer. I try to open my throat for him, but it makes me choke. He ignores this and I enjoy the kick that comes with it, disregarding my right to comfort.

My orgasm becomes more pronounced, and I doubt it takes much to push me over the edge. When he starts masturbating on my face, I rub myself and bring the orgasm to a ticklish climax where "before" meets "after" and "I must not" becomes "I did it". This rush to my head makes my muscles weaken and for those few seconds I ride my orgasm and nothing else exists anymore. My body contracts rhythmically and I scream. I feel his sperm hitting my skin, first hot and then quickly cooling off.

And then it dawns on me - I am a cheater and he has made me his little whore.

THE CEOS WIFE

A colleague of mine was a strange guy with a lot of strange stories from the old days in the steel mill. He had even published a book about life in the steelworks, mostly a book with lots of black and white pictures.

One day we visited a plumbing shop. Some students had a great idea, probably trying to be funny, so they poured cement into the sink on Friday afternoon, and of course the sink had to be replaced.

We went over to the desk to place an order. Behind the desk sat a nice woman in her early fifties. Pretty fit and hot. I could well imagine that she was very hot ten years ago.

Back in the car my colleague was laughing. He said he had seen how I looked at her as if I was a dog and she was a bitch in heat. He laughed at his own remark.

He told me that she was married to the big boss, the CEO, as they call it today, of the old steelworks. The plant where I used to work. She divorced him, five guys, myself included, got fired. I looked at him, he smiled. We fucked her, the big boss found the proof, she divorced him and we got fired.

I looked at him and I laughed. Without saying a word, he started the car and we drove back to our school and the cemented sink.

The next day after lunch he showed me a thick envelope. His hand moved it across the table towards me. He blinked.

I opened it and found a photo album. On the front was a big yellow flashing smiley face. He said these were the unpublished pictures of life in the steel mill.

Page one, a picture of her... a black and white picture. She was dressed nice and neat. Classic skirt and blouse. Just like a secretary. She was hot, she had a beautiful smile, and she had this thing. I find it hard to describe, some women have "sex" written all over them.

He told me that in her younger days she was, and still is, the hottest girl in town. Of course she married the big man at the mill. Rich, big house, but a really boring economist. His humour was as dry as the Sahara, and he could drive a person crazy with boredom after a five minute conversation. But he was good at running the mill.

His wife worked as a coordinator at the mill, booking meetings, fixing conference rooms and so on. She was the opposite of her husband. She flirted, laughed, was happy and sexy.

I turned to the next page in the album. Next picture, also black and white. Her in the middle, light-gray skirt, short tight, white blouse. And two dirty guys in helmets, coveralls and safety shoes. She was laughing, her whole face was laughing.

He went on talking while I looked at the picture, describing how things developed over the years. How her little flirt with the boys evolved from little hints and blinks to more boldness, and how the boys' comments evolved from little comments about her beauty to more direct comments about her body.

Again I opened a new page. In this picture she was standing in front of a desk, leaning forward and holding a pen in her hand. A normal position in an office. Except that her head was turned back and she was smiling, she looked directly into the camera and blinked.

When I looked at the pictures, my colleague told me that he had a good relationship with her. How he was a talented photographer back then and how she enjoyed his attention with the camera and that all the pictures were taken with her permission.

I turned to the next page, I was quite excited. On this page there were two pictures. She was in a mechanical workshop. On the first picture she held a grease gun in one of her hands. She had a devilish smile and a spoonful of grease in the other hand. On the other picture she sent the photographer a teasing smile as she rubbed the grease with her fingers.

When I looked at the pictures, he explained to me how things had developed over the years. How her flirting had become rougher and rougher and how the boys, like in these pictures, introduced her to different things in the workshop. Like the grease gun. How they told her that day before the picture was taken that the fat was Vaseline. And how they responded to her more direct flirting, she responded to her sexual attention. A mutual pleasure is the right words.

I turned to a new page and was curious about the next picture. It was in a break room where the boys were eating their lunch. She was sitting at the table with the boys. I noticed that it was the same boys in all the pictures. Four boys and the photographer. She was holding a banana in her hand and the tip in her mouth.

My assistant continued the conversation, but I didn't listen much.

I quickly turned to a new page. I'm not sure what I expected, but I was not disappointed. There were four pictures, artistic style, and like all pictures in black and white. No colours. The first picture, a dark room, the flash of the camera made her white shirt look very white, a dirty industrial worker hands her the tit. She smiled and looked into the camera. Second picture, another hand on the other tit. Other hand, bigger. Third picture, both hands removed, but her white shirt was not so white anymore. Two dirty handprints on her tits. In the fourth picture, a guy kissed her neck and three others stroked her.

The contrast between her beautiful white and grey clothes and her dirty hands and overalls was fantastic.

My colleague said that this was her game, she was in full control and then he left the room.

I stared at the pictures. I remembered the nice woman in the plumber's workshop. Her smile, nice and polite.

Again I looked at the fourth picture. Her eyes were closed, she leaned with her back against the man who was kissing her neck. Her face was turned upwards towards the ceiling. Her mouth was half open.

On the next page, a picture, it was the workshop. A dirty mattress on the floor. She was on her knees. Still dressed, but not as clean. Four guys around her. She smiled into the camera.

I turned the page. Almost the same picture, but all four had erect penises, and she was holding two in her hand and sucking on one. She wasn't looking into the camera right now.

On the next page, the fourth guy was sitting behind her. He had pulled her skirt up around her waist. His hand was between her legs from behind.

New picture, close to her face. A cock in her mouth, eyes half open, animal lust. The angle of the photo was good, and I could see the fourth guy smiling, and I imagined his fingers deep in her holes.

I closed my eyes. My dick was rock hard. These pictures were much better than a modern digital HD home train.

I flipped to a new page. She was standing, skirt around the waist, shirt around the waist. A hand pulled up her black panties, they were enclosed by her pussy panties. Some other hands pulled her tits and squeezed her nipples.

One hand pulled her head back after her hair, and a finger was in her mouth. I imagined a hard time for her.

In the next picture, scissors cut off her panties and bra. Skirt and shirt still around her waist. She was still held by many hands and because of the view of her nipples they were not tender. She looked down. Whether she was looking at the scissors, the nipples or at what I could not make out. But one thing I could say. She was horny. Her eyes and her mouth could not lie.

I looked at the picture for a long time. Every detail. Her white skin had traces of her dirty hands. Tits red stains from pinching.

My hand turned to a new page. It was lifted by three men. One on each side and one holding her head. It was nice to see how they treated her with care and not at the same time. The fourth man sat between her legs. The face was buried in her crotch. Her nipples were stiff, and the expression on her face made her groan.

New page, new picture. Her pussy, close up. She was glistening. Swollen pussy lips, a swollen clitoris. A dark, hairy finger stuck halfway inside her. Or it was on its way out. glistening from her white, creamy juices.

Next page. She was still held between the fingers. She pulled her hair, raised her head up and looked down herself. The fourth guy was between her legs. He showed her the grease gun and a big grease spot, or Vaseline, on his finger.

I quickly turned to the next page. A picture from a good angle. It shows a knuckle deep in the butt and face. I couldn't remember ever seeing a woman with a hornier expression on her face.

From here it was a series of pictures of her basically getting fucked in every direction, in every hole. They changed positions here, on all fours, on her stomach, riding, on her back. Fucked in the pussy, fucked in the ass, fucked in the mouth, DPed. Certainly sucking the cock that had fucked her in the ass. And cumshots in pussy, ass and mouth. And a really red ass with a distinct handprint.

The last picture was of her lying on the mattress. Exhausted. She was glistening with sweat, semen and salvia. Smiling in a tired, happy way.

I closed the album. Surely I would never be as horny as I am now.

My co-worker entered the room. He smiled. She told me that somehow her husband found out about it, and that was the end of the marriage and our work. These pictures are the only copies, and you're the only one who saw them.

Maybe we should go to the store and visit her one day. He winked at me and smiled.

NEW OFFICE

Despite the various restrictions imposed by the corona virus, I was able to start my new job on Monday, and it had been a hell of a week. I had just finished my last scheduled session on Friday and was thinking about lunch when my phone rang.

"Amy!" I answered happily. "What are you up to?"

"Well, it's been a long time since we've had lunch, and I was curious if you'd like to eat," she said.

"Sure. Where are you?"

"I'm down in your building. After you told me the good news, I thought I'd come out and surprise you."

"Fantastic. I'll be right down," I said, hanging up, grabbing my coat from the back of the door, then walking through the empty office space to the elevator.

I got off the elevator and saw Amy. She was wearing leggings and a sweatshirt with a zipper. Based on past experiences, I could clearly remember the busty figure she was hiding under her humble clothes. Despite the social distance, I gave her a big hug and felt her face and chest pressing against my torso.

"It's good to see you! You look fantastic, as always," I said.

"Thank you," she blushed slightly. "You look good too. All dressed up like a boss," she said, flicking her tie.

"You know me, I'd rather be in a T-shirt and cargo pants. But you gotta do what you gotta do, right? Besides, Lisa likes it," I said in allusion to my wife.

"I bet she does," she said as we headed for the parking garage.

"Where are the children?"

"At home with Sean. I said I needed a ride after being cooped up for so long."

I opened the door for her, and then I put myself in the driver's seat. My dick twitched, remembering the times we fucked in the same car over the years.

We swung by a local gyroscopic joint and we were able to drive off, because all the seats were closed. Since we had nowhere else to go, I suggested we eat in my office. Amy agreed it was the only option that made sense.

We laughed as we remembered it and caught up. Most of our interactions in those days took place through social media where we checked each other out.

"Nice office," she said, looking out of the floor at the windows on the ceiling as I pulled a chair up to the desk and cleared some space for us to eat.

"Yes," I smiled proudly, "it's all right."

We sat and ate and laughed, and the stress of the week disappeared from our minds. Our knees shook a few times, and when she leaned over to steal one of my fries, I stole a peek into her shirt to get a glimpse of her ample cleavage. Once, when she bent down to speak, her hand rested on my thigh just above my knee.

When we finished eating, I leaned back and said, "What a pity we didn't get dessert.

"Maybe we can think of something else," she said, moving her face closer to mine and turning her chair towards me.

"Perhaps..." I leaned towards her repeatedly in silence, my hands sliding up her thighs to her hips and then to her waist.

She wrapped her arms around my neck and our lips met.

I had neglected to kiss Amy. She was such a passionate lover, and it makes cheating, which was true for both of us at the time, even hotter.

Without breaking the kiss, I took one hand and pushed the leftovers of lunch onto the desk, then grabbed them by the hips, picked them up and lifted them up to put them on the desk.

She giggled playfully and pulled me towards her while I pressed my body against her.

To waste no time, I kissed down her neck and my hands moved up her chest, over her sweatshirt that covered her voluptuous bosom. She moaned as I touched her, expressing the same lust that had swollen inside me.

I leaned back and pulled the zipper of her shirt down, revealing her tits covered with a black bra.

"That's so hot, baby," I said and bent over to kiss her cleavage while I held her tits in my hands.

She took off her jacket behind her and then felt her bra loosen as she must have opened it from behind. I let it fall from my hands as I kissed up to one nipple, sucked and nibbled at her and then went to the other, her fingers running through my hair.

I withdrew to kiss her again, our mouths opened, our tongues danced. My hands pulled my tie apart when I felt her hands finding my belt. As I unbuttoned my shirt I felt my zipper come down and then my boxers were pulled down so she could grab my stiff cock.

She stroked me before pushing me back and slipping from the desk to the floor. When she started kissing and licking my naked cock, I took off my shirts and threw them on the floor with the growing pile of clothes.

I moaned loudly as she began to take me in her mouth. My hands rested in her hair and held it out of the way as she started to bob.

"I missed your mouth," I said, my eyes closed and my head tilted back as she teetered and sucked and licked me.

There was a popping sound as she pulled her head off my cock.

"I missed sucking you," she said, and then went back to him.

As much as I wanted her to go on for hours, I knew our time was running out, so I pulled her up and turned her over to the desk. I grabbed her leggings and panties and pulled her down by her shapely legs while she looked at me hungrily over her shoulder.

I laid my cock at the entrance of her already soaked pussy and pressed my head inside. Amy moaned loudly as she laid her head on the desk.

I slowly rocked into her, enjoying the feeling of her pussy, which was intensified by the sound of her squeaking and moaning. In a short time I was deeply buried with my balls and enjoyed a pussy I had not had for years.

"Baby, you feel so good," I said as I picked up speed.

"Moooooorrrreee", she moaned as she came on my cock.

I pulled it out, turned it around, put it on the desk and dived back into it.

Her tits bounced and giggled on her chest as I stomped off.

"Sperm, please," she moaned. "I need it in me."

The feeling was so incredible I wanted to fuck her against the window, but I couldn't deny her what she wanted.

"Ahhhhh," I moaned loudly as I came in her spurt after spurt, my hands holding her hips.

"My God", I said, my head tilted back, my cock still stuck in her pussy.

"I missed you," she said, "but I really missed that."

I pulled back and sat in the chair.

"Do you want to clean me up?" I asked with a grin.

Moaning, she fell back on her knees in front of me and took my soft cock in her mouth, sucked it carefully and licked it clean.

"I wanted to fuck you against the mirror."

"I wanted that too," Amy replied. "Maybe next lunch," she said before putting me back in her mouth.

NEW CAR

Jasmine and I left the restaurant laughing.

Jasmine: I have a new car.

Me: You got rid of the Subaru?

Jasmine held up the keys: Yes, since my mother-in-law lives with us and romps around with the kids, I needed something bigger. It's a Volvo. It's nice.

Me: Better than the Subaru?

Jasmine, laugh: I hated the Subaru.

Me, reaching for the keys: Let me see.

She gives them to me as we walk over. I unlock and look inside: Spacious. You could take a nap in here. (We laugh.) How does she handle it?

With Jasmine: She's fine. I like her.

Me: Can I take it for a quick spin?

Jasmin: Jasmin: Do you have time?

Me, looking at my watch and smiling: It will be alright.

Jasmine: It will be all right.

I climb into the driver's seat while Jasmine gets in on the passenger side. I take the opportunity to look at her legs and feel myself getting stiff.

I start the car and put the SUV in reverse. The Volvo drives gently out of the curve. I start the car and leave the parking lot.

Me: That's nice. How much is it?

Jasmine: 43

Me: Not bad.

I'm walking straight down the street where our old office used to be.

Me: You rented out the old room. It's now the headquarters of some bank.

Jasmine: Cool.

Me: There's our old place. Should I stop over there?

Jasmine: You are so bad.

Me: Well, you were wearing a dress...

I put my hand on her thigh and press her hem slightly upwards.

Jasmine: I was wondering when you were going to say something about that.

Her eye blinks as her mischievous grin grows.

I turn into the parking lot where we park after work and walk towards the shady spot.

Jasmine: I can't. You have to go to work and I have to go home.

Me: Just for a minute?

Jasmine (grinning and biting her lip): Just for one minute?

I'll park the car and leave it running.

Me: (winking): Yeah, just for a minute.

I lean forward as she leans in, our lips kiss. No sooner was the contact established than she grabs me and pulls me towards her. My hand continues to slide up her thigh and my other hand grabs her hip. She pushes herself towards me and pulls me closer to her over the centre console.

I (breaks our kiss): Let's see how big her back is.

Jasmine, her breath ripping, moans approvingly and climbs over the centre console and into my back. I take off my suit jacket and climb back following her.

Without any loss of time she immediately climbs onto my lap and kisses me. My hands grab her ass and pull her further on me. Her double-Ds are pressed against me.

My dick is pressed against my pants.

My hands move up her sides and find their way to her chest. She moans into my mouth.

Jasmine: I dream of it.

Me: Me too.

One of my hands is rubbing her nipple through her dress, while the other is returning to her thigh and pushing her dress up on the way to her panties.

She's rubbing up against me.

Me: You're rubbing my pants.

Jasmine: I'm sorry, Jasmine. (She continues to crunch.)

Me: Let me help.

I kiss her deep and then move her from my lap. I reach down to loosen my belt, but she is already grabbing my zipper. As I undo my button, she reaches into my boxers and grabs my cock.

Jasmine: I missed that...

She starts to caress me.

I pull down my pants and she lets go of me for a moment. As soon as my pants are down, I lean back and she bends over to suck me into her mouth.

Me, by my moaning: I missed your mouth.

My left hand rests on her head as she bounces and sucks while my right hand reaches around to caress her chest.

Without removing her mouth, she climbs up and puts her knees on the seat. My right hand pulls up her dress and I put my hand on her panty-covered ass and squeeze her.

Me: This is so good...

I pull down her panties on her thighs and put my hand on her dripping pussy.

She's shaking and pulling her mouth away from me to moan.

Me: Come here.

I pull her up and kiss her. She slides closer to me.

Me: Climb up.

I: Jasmine: Please...

She sits on me and lowers herself down on my cock. My hands are on her hips under her dress, while I make sure she doesn't go too fast and enjoys every inch as she slides down.

Jasmine (begging): Please...

I pull her down and fill her up.

Jasmine: Thank you. I needed this so much.

She swayed her hips as she snuggled against me.

Jasmine: So good, so good...

Me: You feel incredible.

I push into her while she rocks against me. I hear her breathing faster and then she hums.

Her body trembles as she pauses for a moment while I am buried deep inside her.

Jasmin: That was amazing!

Me: More?

Jasmine: Jasmine: You cannot come inside me.

Me: Okay.

I turn us around and lay her down and climb on her. I hammer my only regret into her that we don't have time to take off her dress and let me fuck her tits.

Jasmine, moans quickly as she builds to another climax. She shudders at me again as I look further inside her.

Me: I'm going to cum. Where to?

Jasmine: In my mouth.

She presses herself against me and while I lean back, she climbs back on her knees and lifts her butt up into the air. She devours me while I put my finger in her dripping pussy.

As she keeps sucking and bobbing, I push myself up to meet her here. My hands move to the back of her head and help to guide her in an original way.

Me: Here I come.

My back arches and she intensifies her sucking while my tail stutters. She continues sucking until I lean back and take my hands off her head. She swallows my semen while I breathe.

Jasmine: I have to go now.

Me, looking at my watch: I have to go too.

We adjust ourselves and climb forward again.

I, while we are retreating, put my hand on her thigh: That was great. Thank you.

Jasmin: Thank you. I needed that so much.

Me: So, can you have lunch again next week?

Jasmine, grinning: Maybe.

BED REVIEW

I took a photo of the pendant on the bed and sent it to you with the message: "Your wife said she loves my bed".

You would understand it as the picking up boys do to each other all the time, if you would just perceive it in such a way that I am referring to the time when she had slept there, when she lived with her sister and we were all out and about, or when you both had slept there while you were babysitting for my wife and me. You have no idea that we had collapsed in a pile of wrapped limbs on top of each other after we'd been fucking hard for a morning or an afternoon.

But we hadn't just shagged in my bed. We used every opportunity to steal a quick fuck. We'd done it once, when we went to get everyone coffee. And every time we had lunch together, now that our offices were within walking distance, we'd wet my cock. Your bed was best when you were downstairs with her family and we had put our respective children to sleep.

Sometimes these were quick naps where I would take him deep and fast and leave her with a pussy full of cum. Another time we took our time and I enjoyed every inch of her petite body.

And I know you don't make her blow you because she thinks it's not right for a man and a woman to do it, but I do. We're already doing so much wrong that I make her suck my dick like she's drowning and it's full of air. She's a natural. I took it from her bubbly personality that she'll be a donor, and I've not been disappointed.

And these secrets we share, like the fact that you cheated on her once in the lounge or the secret trips to the strip club? Well, she knows, and let me tell you, kid, she fucks well when she wants revenge.

She wanted to confront you, but I knew a better way for her to get back at you, and that clearly had something to do with her setting me up. But I couldn't just tell her that. I had to convince her myself.

So over several days, over lunch and text messages, I led her down a trail of crumbs. We talked about how you were the only man she'd been with, and that you were probably who you always were, and that you wouldn't change. We talked about the effects of divorce on the children and how upset her parents would be. We talked about how she was just trying to get over it, and that no matter how much time passed, every time she looked at you, she would still see your infidelity. We talked about revenge, but how nothing she did to you would ever equal that.

That's when I told her it was really about how she felt. If she agreed to get over it, it would only affect her, just like if she didn't. So I told her to do what would make her feel better, even if she was the only one who knew.

At the end of this lunch she gave me a big, tight hug, the first time she really pressed her body against me and let me feel her breasts bouncing against me. She thanked me and we planned to have lunch tomorrow.

The next day she seemed nervous and a little awkward. At first she said that everything was fine, but when I pushed her, she finally decided that she had decided what to do, but she needed my help. I told her that I would do whatever I had to do because I just wanted her to be happy.

She kept telling me that she had never been with anyone else but you and that she had never seen anyone else, she hesitated to see her naked before. She decided that she wanted to take revenge, even if you never knew, because it was about how she felt about it, as I had said. So she looked at her phone and then back at me and told me she was ready.

My phone beeped, and I noticed that I received a series of messages. When I looked, I saw that they were pictures of her from her bathroom at home. As I flipped through the pictures, she had less and less to see in each one, so she absorbed the digital striptease she was playing to me.

I let my excitement and attraction show on my face when I finally looked at her nude photo. I tried to burn every inch of her sexy body into my memory, from her shaved hill to her sassy tits to her aroused nipples. I was careful to bite my lip when I looked up from my phone. As I looked up from my phone, my eyes slowly moved up her body, clearly undressing her before me.

She was crimson, and I knew that in this situation I had to strengthen her self-confidence. I began by telling her how beautiful she was, how amazing her body was and how amazingly brave she was to take this step. I laid my hand on hers when I told her how much it meant to me that she trusted me and decided that I could be trusted too.

She relaxed and held my hand and thanked me again for all the help I gave her and my support. We ended the lunch with many flirtatious looks from her and I made it clear that I was taking a close look at her. After we finished our lunch, I took her back to her office as usual, only that I took every opportunity to finally check her out openly.

The next day we met again and again for lunch, and again and again she sent me a set of pictures, this time in sexy lingerie, with her undressing. The next day it was the same and this time in different underwear. And every day more cleavage was shown, so that I could see with my own two eyes what I could only see on pictures before. Every day I made sure that I let her know how beautiful and brave she was.

On Friday, after another series of lingerie strip photos and a flirtatious lunch, she took me back to her office by a different route. When we arrived at a place where nobody was around, she hugged me again and then leaned over for a kiss. That was our first kiss, deep and passionate, and I finally had the opportunity to grab her ass and squeeze it while we kissed.

When my wife and I came to your house this weekend, we both pretended that nothing was going on and nobody seemed to notice, especially you.

On Monday at lunch she took me to her car instead of our regular place. As soon as we entered the elevator of the parking garage, I couldn't help but wrap my arms around her. We kissed angrily, both of us persisting in our hunger and passion for the other. Only when the elevator door closed after we reached our floor did we stop our kiss, although no one got out. We pressed the button to go back, but it was too late, our elevator had been called to another floor. We did our best not to laugh so much when the other person got in and the three of us returned to their floor.

After we got off, she led us to her cabin, stealing an occasional kiss and I grabbed her waist or butt. When we arrived at the car, I lifted her onto the hood, wrapped her in my arms and made out with her, pulling me against her with her legs and arms, hitting me with as much of her body as possible.

She broke our embrace and told me we should get in the car. I gladly did her the favor of letting her climb into the back seat and pat her butt as she continued to crawl in front of me. I climbed in and sat down next to her but before I even sat down we were hugged again. My hands were finally really free to stroke her body.

My hands found a way under her shirts, touched her naked skin for the first time and I could hear her breathing. I pushed my hands up, felt her flat stomach and rubbed her back. We had leaned closer together, practically over each other.

I pulled her onto my lap, and because of her petite size she had some headroom. My hard cock was now pressed against her pussy, closer than ever, despite our pants and underwear. I twitched it against her and heard her moaning again.

I pulled her shirts up and she forced me to let her take them off. I took a moment to feast on her white bra-clad breast before kissing, licking and massaging her. You are a lucky man.

She undid her bra and dropped it when she bumped into me. She must have been so aroused because it only took a few minutes before she played with her tits, kissed and crunched them. It was a pleasant surprise, especially how overwhelmed she seemed by the experience. Later I learned from her that this was her first orgasm. Of course it was not her last.

After she had come, she insisted on taking care of me as well, so she slipped off my lap and sat down next to me. I let her unduly drop my pants and helped her to let them slide down. I was rock hard and she couldn't help mentioning that I was taller than you.

She started to caress me and when I encouraged her to take it in her mouth, she apologized that she was no good because she only did it a few times. It's really your loss.

I've had girls in the past who were never that good, and here she rocks my world. And to top it off, when I blew my load, she didn't even pause. She swallowed that shit. I complimented her on her skill, which made her blush. It was just the first of many blowjobs she gave me, either as her main event or as a prelude.

We finally did it a few days later. We both called in sick and got a hotel room instead. She really dressed up for the event, with her make-up and lingerie, a new set she had bought just for me.

I fucked here in every position imaginable, which was an experience for her, considering she told me that you only do a few punches and a grunt. She loves to drive, which works well, considering how many times we've done it in cars.

She also loves the puppy, which also worked to our advantage, because she is adventurous and has the potential to get caught in public. We have banged in parks, parking garages, family bathrooms and even a few times in the woods. The craziest ones were of course in one of our houses, in the middle of the night, when we sneak into the kitchen or living room and do a quickie.

Anyway, that first day really set the bar. I must have injected into her five or six times, and one of them was in her mouth. I remember that because she came when I came in her mouth. Unbelievable.

We only snuck away a couple of times for a whole day, I'd like to do more, but we only have so much time. And I think we should do it soon, considering you've been talking about having another baby. While it's exciting to think about getting her pregnant, I'm sure that everyone would realize that it's my child.

Anyway, I look forward to fucking her in your new bed.

THE NEW ADMIN

WOW a new girl in the office. I am speechless.

"Hello" is all I can do with a little smile.

Man, it's hot in here, it must be me. She is hot. Slim, petite, with a nice smile. Small, perfect tits, hot legs. Uhhhhh... what did I come here for? Oh right, I need to speak to your boss. With one last smile on the new girl and she goes back to the shop to fix more equipment. The rest of the day I'm locked in a daydream dreaming about seducing this beautiful woman, but I noticed a ring. I'm not a cheater, but damn it, I could cheat with her!

My daydream is a distraction because it goes on every time I see her. The seduction would be so sweet. For the past few days, I can't even remember her name. Her boss is an ass and doesn't formally introduce new employees. Finally I find out that her name is Nat. Natalie.

The daydream grows more vivid as we talk over the next few weeks. I wonder if she caught me staring at her in a daze. Hey, pumpkin, get a grip. You don't have a chance, you're both involved with other people. Days go by, but my imagination of her seduction doesn't fade. I learn more about her and her life. She may not seem like a cheating girl, but a boy can dream.

It would begin at a place we both agreed upon...

Hot kisses and caresses. I lead her into the shower, our hands gliding over each other's bodies as I sensually pull off her skirt and low-cut blouse while the hot water in the bathroom rises steaming. I fiddle with my clothes while she undresses them hungrily. I turn her around and bring my hands around her neck to her shoulders and down the sides to her hips and pull her close to me. She raises her arms and wraps her hands around my head and neck. I kiss her just below the ear and pull kisses down to the shoulders while taking the bra strap first from one shoulder and then from the other. I put my hands around her sides and clasp her beautiful breasts tightly. She pants and emits a small groan while I pull her towards me and pinch her neck together. She lowers her hands to my sides and pulls my hips closer to my hips, rubbing her butt against my erection. Now it's my turn to moan.

One sharp inhale: "Natalie."

"Mmm, I like the way you say my name. You make it sound so sexy. Say it again."

And then a muffled whisper. Natalie.

She turns to me without breaking off contact. I brush her hair back and wrap my fingers around her with one hand, the other holding her tight little back against me. I lead her face upwards, exposing her neck, leaning in for a kiss just below her jawbone and moving slowly towards her collarbone. I bite gently while opening her bra and throwing it to the side.

We move into the waiting hot water and let it pour over us. She puts her hands around my head and pulls me to her chest to get the attention I need. Slowly I lick her nipple and take it in my mouth. Natalie moans a little and I feel her tremble. I move to the other nipple and she trembles again, pressing my mouth even harder into her breast.

"You're driving me crazy," she moans.

"Well, you've been driving me crazy for weeks, and now I finally have you. I guess a little payback is in order."

I start hauling kisses into her navel. Natalie writhes and lets out a little giggle. She pulls me back to eye level to show me the desire in her eyes. We pour the hot water over each other as we explore each other with our hands. I grab some soap and quickly lather up something to make us nice and slippery. I press her against the shower wall and attack her neck again. She lifts her leg around my hip to drag her smooth hill against my throbbing cock. The feeling she has against me is electric and I am ready to come from the heat of our passion to orgasm. I need more. My desire to hear this beautiful woman in orgasm is overwhelming. I pull her tightly against me and start kissing and licking me to her navy as I pour the hot water over us. I put her leg over my shoulder and get a first glimpse of her most private area. I put a kiss just over her hill and slowly pull my lips towards her beautiful clitoris. I split her swollen lips to expose her clitoris. She pants and pushes her fingers into my hair and leads me to where she needs more attention. I lick her clitoris and close my lips around the delicious little bud and suck gently.

"AHHHH Fuck". No more quips. I want you."

"Not yet." I tell her while I slip two fingers inside her pussy and roll her up to rub her G-spot.

"Ahh." She gasps. "I need to feel you."

"MMM. "No, I want you to come for me first." As I continue to rub her G-spot and put my mouth back on her clit and twirl my tongue around and start sucking on that delicious little nub.

"Please!" She's begging me. "I'll be right there."

I look up at her with a smile. "Come for me, Natalie. I want you to come just for me."

I come back to lick her nectar. Her body cramps as her pussy squeezes my fingers and I feel a warm flood wash into my waiting mouth.

"MMMMMM FUCK, I want you so much," she screams.

She pulls my hair and tears me from the beautiful pussy that gave me pleasure. She lifts me up until our eyes meet.

"Take me to bed" while she wraps both legs around my waist and her arms around my neck and holds me tight. She pulls my head back and nibbles my neck, and the electricity of her touch weakens my knees as I fiddle with the shower door to carry her to the waiting bed. I sit her down on the corner and gently lay her feet on the floor. She loosens her grip, but tries to pull me close to her.

I tear myself away from the hot kisses she demands and slide down her hot body, kisses after, until I stare at her beautiful pussy again. I put her hot little feet on my shoulders and expose her all over me. I kiss the tender spot where her thigh meets her body.

Natalie moans." God, you make me so aroused. I want your cock inside me. I need you now."

"I'm sorry, Natalie. I want to see you cum. I want to taste your sweet nectar when you come for me.

"Mmm, I like the way you say my name. That is so sexy. I don't usually use my full name, but it gives me goose bumps when you say it."

"Mmmm... Natalie."

I moan in her beautiful pussy and slide my tongue from her entrance to the top of her hill. She breathes in small breaths through clenched teeth as I use my fingers to spread the hood around her swollen clit and wrap my mouth around it. I nibble at her, taking care not to bite too hard. Her fingers are intertwined in the sheets as she screams

"Ahh FUCK... Enough!"

She pushes me away with her feet until I'm on the ground, and then she slams on top of me and pushes me down. She pulls my nails into my chest as she spreads my hips.

"Now it's my turn to tease her." She tells me so, a smile on her face, her eyes burning with desire.

She slides her fingernails across my chest and then down my arms. Our fingers entwine as she scratches her pussy on my cock. She glides along without allowing me to reach her entrance. Her touch is electric as I feel the heat of her gorgeous pussy almost making me let go.

"Ahh... Natalie, you're making me cum."

A wicked grin spreads across her beautiful face.

"Not so funny when we tease, is it? Now it's my turn to get what I want."

Natalie rolls her hips and bends over to guide my cock into her pussy. She slowly descends on me. Now it's my turn to gasp and shake.

"Oh my God, you're so perfect." I moan. "Tease me. Please me. Use me. Use me."

She leans over and bites my earlobe.

"I need you deep inside me. I want to feel you coming."

Natalie starts rubbing up against me and I can feel her cervix pressing against the tip of my dick.

"Ahh... you're so deep. I want you so much."

She moves forward until only the tip of my dick is left in her, then she pushes her pussy back and pushes our pubes together. The pace accelerates with long, full blows. Our breathing comes panting and moaning as our hunger increases. I adapt to her blows. She digs her nails into my chest.

The excitement with which she takes control is electric as I place my hands on her breasts to gently press her nipples between my fingers and apply pressure until she moans. She slides her hands up my chest and bends forward, crossing her arms behind my head and holding my hands on her nipples. I lift my hips according to her strokes and let the pressure build. I can feel her excitement. The pressure is almost unbearable.

"Mmm. Natalie, I'll be right there."

"Oh, yeah... come inside me. I want to cum with you. I wanna feel you."

I push hard in her pussy and I rub my cock deep, my pubic bone against hers. I can feel her pussy tightening and I'm swaying my hips.

"Oh YES", she screams.

I can't hold myself back any longer because this familiar rush goes right through me.

"Ahh Natalie." I scream as I try to pull her hips even closer to mine.

She makes a deep groan and trembles as I let go deep inside her. She leans back and digs her fingers into my hair and pulls my head against her breasts. I move my hands to bite her nipple and she screams as her pussy contracts and milk every drop of me.

We break down with her on my writhing chest and let her hair fall around us and wrap ourselves in a hot, sweaty cocoon.

"Wow," she says and whispers hoarsely, "How about an encore?"

CHEATING YOUNG GIRLFRIEND

Ever since we met in college, I've been warning myself about what other people would say about my girlfriend. As a nineteen-year-old sophomore, Annabelle was the girl who seemed innocent until you met her. I had known her since the late freshman year of high school and had witnessed her blossoming within two or three years from a clumsy young petite blonde with no sexual experience to an extremely sexually mature young petite blonde.

When I started courting Annabelle in my last year of school, she was a virgin with little appetite for sex. After I had seen her for about two years, she had transformed into an unprecedented level of sexual appetite and fervour. As a strapping, young, petite blonde, Annabelle had limited herself, and I knew it. My craving for porn and erotic stories finally made me succumb and attracted her. At first it started quite innocently, with my own subconscious urging us to play different scenarios. We started with the most obvious scenarios, such as the messenger and the bored housewife. After some basic nudges, Annabelle started to enter these role-plays each time with an extremely wet center. I started testing her sexual boundaries with my hands and fist until I could no longer nudge her with my fingers or penis alone. However, her favorite role-playing game took place towards the end of her climax and involved a hypothetical large penis penetrating her and killing her.

On a whim, I used a debit card that my grandmother had given me for Christmas to buy a toy for Annabelle and me to play with as we rang in the New Year. My mistake was ordering her toy while I blacked out drunk at a Christmas party. The party had caused me to miss the 22nd with Annabelle and my family. Annabelle added to my frustration by sending me a picture of her in red underwear and matching bra, fucking the fake Christmas tree we bought. When I looked at this photo and drank a bottle of liquor at my desk, I suddenly had a tendency to order sexual toys. A few clicks further on I realized that her "present" had no chance to arrive until Christmas and still ordered the most realistic but inconspicuous dildo I could find in a drunken stupor. In my drunken state I thought I had ordered a soft looking pink dildo that Annabelle could play with in front of me.

Instead I had somehow ordered a realistic black cyberskin dildo. Amazon only made me aware of the difference in memory when the package arrived. Ashamed, I checked my phone on Christmas Eve and saw the recent delivery. I checked my drunk purchase and was ashamed. Hoping to return it, I created a return option since I had finished work for the day. Without my knowledge at the time, my girlfriend had knocked on the door half-naked and signed for the box. Without thinking, my girlfriend took the box into her bedroom and opened it, thinking the contents were a BLU Ray or Xbox controller. Instead, the plastic lining of the cyberskin dildos revealed itself, and without thinking, she tore open the box. With little interest, but much remorseful horniness, Annabelle spent the next few hours exploring the inside of the packaging on her own. Towards the end of the working day I checked my account again and saw that the package had been delivered. I clicked on the product details and saw first hand my drunken mistake. The sexual toy I had ordered for my young girlfriend and me to experiment with was 9" long and simulated the size of a real BBC. I checked the shipping details and was shocked to learn that it had been updated to show that it had been delivered to the front door.

Instead of dealing head-on with the impending "delivery", I let the problem resolve itself naturally. Without the actual dildo product, I naturally assumed that the "misdirected" toy had been delivered to the wrong address, and I continued with my normal life when I received my credit note in early

January. During a fairly routine dive into the issues of the year, I saw the delivery of the toy. As Annabelle went into the store, I rummaged through the walk-in closet, expecting to find nothing but curiosity. After looking around briefly, I found the black cyberskin dildo. I suspected it had been lost, but inspected it more deeply, found it smelling of sexual fluids and stowed it away.

I decided to ignore the find and let the toy walk around the bedroom apparently without my knowledge. This went on for 2-3 months until my girlfriend used my laptop for a project and forgot to log off. Not only did she forget to log out of the course website, but Annabelle also forgot to log out of her Apple ID and the media and the following photos were synchronized. Knowing that the deadline was tight, I searched her computer while she was using the toilet. In just a few minutes I had logged into her website and checked the results. Not only did Annabelle have an Adult Friend Finder account that filled automatically, but several other dating sites showed up. Curiously, I checked each address in her browsing history and loaded the associated websites.

Nineteen-year-old Annabelle not only had pictures sent to her by other people, but she also had sexually suggestive pictures on each of the profiles I flipped through. Strangely enough, my penis hardened when I looked through my girlfriend's robust search history and remained erect the whole time. Never before had I been fascinated by the thought that my girlfriend's vagina had been "misplaced" and enjoyed by someone else. But the thought crossed my mind as I poked around on my laptop. Finally I could no longer hold the thought back when I found the 9 inch cyberskin dildo in Annabelle's panty drawer. I got into the panty drawer almost immediately. I came almost immediately after discovering it, but hid it from myself. I now saw the length and circumference that only a toy of this size could have. I continued to place the big dildo in the usual place and was amazed every time I could secretly pick it up and insert it into Annabelle while we were having normal sex.

Almost three months after Griffin began to notice that Annabelle was coming home with an increasingly less tight interior, he became surprisingly wise. And yet, as the relationship between Annabelle and Griffin changed, no one spoke directly about the difference. That is, until the discovery that would change their deep and painstakingly managed relationship forever. One afternoon, I came back early and parked my car in the driveway. I walked from the garage into the living room and heard the unmistakable sound of moaning. Instead of feeling my blood boiling and my face glowing red all by itself, I held on to that feeling and continued to listen to the muffled moaning and screaming. Instead of attacking the source of the animal noises I stood in the entrance and listened apparently forever.

Finally I was overwhelmed by the source of the noises and I crept quietly up to the master bedroom. When I reached the top of the stairs, I was struck by the depth and extent of the infidelity that was occurring at that moment. My typically shy girlfriend was lying splayed on my desk when a tall black gentleman stood between her legs and kept pushing forward.

I watched in shock as every second at least seven centimetres of hard black penis rammed into my young white girlfriend. I could see Annabelle's face from my vantage point and it was clear that she was contributing to most of the satisfying sounds. Instead of interrupting the action, I hid and tugged at my penis when my little friend finally came and pulled out the black cock and shot across Annabelle's face and mouth for almost a full minute. Watching the thick ropes of cum cloud my sweet girlfriend's face proved to be too much for me, and I soon lost my short blows. In no time at all I was left standing onmy side while my girlfriend went to a restaurant to eat with the big black man while she was covered with his sperm and did not respond to my own text messages.

ETERNITY IN A MOMENT

Alli chatted with Nick for a few weeks. They had had a social conversation the Sunday before, and she was a little surprised that she wanted to meet him. More surprised that after seeing her, he seemed more attracted to her than ever. She had called him "Sir" a few times and knew that he loved that - he called her "Kitten" by now - partly because her screen name contained "Cat", but also because of the Snapchat filter photos she had sent him, which always had cat ears on them.

She had been reading his stories for weeks and was so incredibly turned on by them - now she was just turned on talking to him and had found herself incredibly horny after their conversation on Sunday. They were both married but frustrated - she thought she was practically a virgin - she had only ever been with her husband, had only ever felt touched by one person and longed to explore. He was naughty, perverse and had an evil side that excited her.

In the beginning she had only chatted and sent stories and occasionally a teasing photo that she had sent him. But lately she had found out that he had given her some orders and she enjoyed obeying him. Then he had asked for a hug and told her how much he had longed to kiss her. She was conflicted - she had never cheated on him, but with Nick she was tempted and excited. They were in the same boat, eyes open and not out to fall in love - just explore some naughty fun together. She decided to meet him for a talk and a hug and see how things went. They had agreed that if she called him sir while she was with him, he could kiss her.

The morning of the meeting dawned bright and clear - she was curled up in bed when Sir's "good morning" message arrived. He again said cheeky and nice things that made her smile, then he sent a photo of "what she had done to him". Fucking - his dick looked thick... she felt the wetness start between her legs, announcing the need to be fucked. She flirted a little, then finally got up and moved. He sent her some stories to start her day off. She hurried around knowing that she had to leave soon, half of her clothes were packed when she suddenly noticed that she didn't wear panties - it wouldn't be the first time she went without, so she put on the pink bra she liked, her black dress and leggings and headed off to work.

The next few hours seemed to drag on, she felt horny and nervous and insecure at the same time. Both were working, so there was little news. She tried to concentrate on her work, but was distracted again and again as she checked her phone, remembered the look on his tail, how wicked his imagination was and wondered how far she was ready to go this afternoon. Lunch arrived and they talked, he sent more stories she hadn't read just yet - she was horny enough already. But his words calmed her down - she knew he wouldn't pressure her, so she was looking forward to seeing him. She mentioned the missing panties to him, and his predictable reaction almost made her giggle.

Back to work for another hour or two, and then it was time. She made her way down-stairs - full of doubts and some nagging insecurities - did he really like her as much as he said? Could she go through with it? When she came home from work, he told her where to go and she walked around the building to the little side street where she could see his car. Slowly she walked to the car and remained determined as she reached the car, opened the door and slipped in next to him. He smiled cheerfully and greeted her cheer-fully with the words she learned to love... "Hello, kittens."

Hello", she managed to get out - she felt the nerves and horniness fighting inside her - he asked her if she wanted a hug and she decided that this was exactly what she needed at that moment. She leaned over to him and felt his arms hug her. She was protective and at the same time comforting and arousing. She began to relax a little. She smiled at his remark that she smelled good. His fingers caressed her arm and back through the mate-rial of her top. She wasn't sure, but she thought she felt him almost kissing her crown and then pulling back. They talked briefly about their work and the chaos there after some outside visitors. Then he asked about the stories - she explained that she hadn't read any of today's yet, and he suggested - quite firmly - that she read one of them now.

She felt her shyness pressing to the fore, but decided to obey him. She turned away so that she would not look at him while reading, opened one of his stories on the phone and started reading. As she did so, she felt his fingers gently on her neck - stroking in slow, gentle circles. When he asked her if it was okay, she sighed in agreement - it felt good on her neck after the stress and chaos of the last few days - but it distracted her and didn't help her horniness at all. She started to read and felt that the low throbbing excitement turned into a fire. She squeezed her legs together and wondered if he had noticed her deeper breathing and the changes she was trying to mask as she felt the need burning inside her. She wanted to kiss him. Shit - she wanted to do more than kiss him, but would she be able to handle it afterwards?

She decided not to read the second story just then - she couldn't really concentrate on it anyway. She slipped into his arms, rolled against him while he held her - the two thoughts arguing back and forth in her head. His soft words in her ear reassured her that there was no pressure, that they could just do what they were doing and that he would be happy. He could be, but would she be? The conversation revolved around his stories and the

adjustment he had made to the previous meeting - where he had turned a friendly encounter into something evil, and she had loved it. He whispered softly in her ear what he would write about today's meeting, and she moaned softly - the fantasy sounded so good - but would reality be any better?

He asked if she was really not wearing panties, and with a cheeky grin she pulled down the edge of her leggings to show her bare hips and waist. This time it was his turn to moan - the word "fuck" slipped gently from between his lips. When she said she was also wearing the pink bra she knew he loved the photo, and he said, "Prove it," she smiled with a slightly cheeky grin and pulled her dress all the way up to show the gorgeous bra and breasts she knew he loved.

Now she could see the lust burning in his eyes and she was so aroused. They talked - cautiously above expectations - it wasn't about love or about hurting anyone - it was two people who were inquiring and trying to do it in a safe way. She looked at him, his eyes, his smile, the gentle firmness with which he had encouraged her, while at the same time taking care not to be pushed or pressured. "Yes, sir..." she whispered. His arms slid around her and his lips met hers. She was soft, searching... the first time she had kissed anyone but her husband. It tasted different, but good. Her lips met and explored, his hand slipped over her soft skin - it felt like an eternity to her, but there was no dramatic outcry in her head. Just the desire to go on - to explore more.

Nick slowly pulled away and smiled at her - she knew how much he wanted it. His gentle words telling her she was a great kisser made her smile. He bent over again and she kissed him eagerly once more. They stayed like that for a while - ignoring the two or three cars that passed them. This time, when he broke the kiss, he undoubtedly knew how to turn her on. His soft voice reminded her that she had to be back at work soon. Then he asked a question she didn't dare answer.

"Is there anything else you'd like me to do before you leave Kitten?"

Fuuuuuck... there was so much she wished for - but she shouldn't go so quickly - should she? In a deep and shy voice she asked him to play with her breasts.

His hand quickly slipped up her dress and lifted it. His deft hands scooped her breast from the cup of the bra - his fingers teasing and pinching her nipples. Her need was now almost too great. She did not think beyond how amazing it felt. Then she felt his fingers caressing her legg-covered pussy and his apology. She didn't want his apology - she wanted his fingers. He had said he wouldn't go that far today, but she needed him to do it, and the way her body reacted to him, she knew he knew it too. So when his whispered voice asked him if she wanted his fingers on her clitoris, she answered immediately with the "Yes Sir", which she knew he would like to hear.

They were with her in a moment, slipped between her soaking wet pussy and found her clitoris in seconds. He knew what he was doing and in a few moments she had her first orgasm. She came, on the fingers of another man, in his car, in the middle of the day in a side street in the city. That was the naughtiest thing she had done in her life. She exploded to a second orgasm. She could have squirted further and further, but Nick suddenly pointed out the time - he didn't want her to get into trouble - and if she was any later, she would be. He pulled his fingers back and held her gently in his arms as she came down. She couldn't believe what she had done, but she didn't regret it. It had been amazing - and she felt that it was only the beginning.

CARRYING ANOTHER MANS SEED

It starts in my bedroom. It's a weekday morning and you've been there for two hours. You've already come inside me twice.

Now you sit on the edge of the bed and I kneel between your legs and I use my mouth and tongue for your cock, balls, stains and asshole.

For 20 minutes now I've been using my tongue and mouth to make your semi hard cock hard enough so you can try again to get what's left in your balls into my pussy. I'm starting to feel your frustration with my inability to get you hard again by seeing how you started grabbing my head and saying the things you started to say. You're also deeply frustrated that I'm not carrying your baby yet.

We were screwing for about 10 weeks at this point. We managed to meet a few times at my apartment, one night at a hotel and surprisingly many times in bathrooms and changing rooms. All together you managed to come inside me over 30 times, but it didn't work out.

The situation has worsened as we have moved forward. Originally, we both injected so violently within minutes, but given the sheer amount of sex in such a short time and the danger and risk, we both really increased what we were both willing to do.

Even this morning, when I opened the door, instead of telling me something, you just grabbed me, squeezed me over the back of my couch and stuck your cock inside me. I had learned by then not to bother me with underwear because it would just get torn off my body, or with your frustration when I wasn't wearing a dress or skirt in those bathrooms. You come into me quickly and roughly from behind.

Your cock continues to pulsate and you push deeper into me to make sure that you fill me as much as possible. You have wrapped my hair around your fist and still haven't let go.

Finally you pull back and tell me to get ready for the next round. Put on the white underwear and white stockings and prepare myself for a time that will not come easily.

In the last weeks the physicality of our relationship has really started to intensify. It took more than a month, but you have finally found and exceeded my limits and boundaries. The first time you managed to do this was in our night at the W-Hotel in the city centre, where you brought me to the ground by the combination of belt and riding whip and I said our safe word.

You were very happy at that moment and quickly climbed up and got inside me while I was lying helplessly on the bed. Your only concern that night was that my screams before you gagged me would cause someone to call the reception or that the marks you left on my body would arouse suspicion in my husband.

Today it would be no different, and after you had roughly taken off your underwear and left only your stockings, you tied me to the bed face down with my bottom in the air. At first you slowly use the leather whip we bought weeks ago on my ass, pussy and legs. You can still see some of your semen when it comes out of my insides.

In the beginning I only move my body away from the whip, but in the end, when I break and can't anymore, you use all your power on me.

This time there is no gag and you are happy about my squeaking and screaming. Of course, that made you rock hard, and you quickly mount me from behind. My moaning and pleading for you to put a baby in me makes you even harder. You tell me that you make me "scream louder now than in 9 months when the baby suckles". You stop deep down inside when your whole weight is on me.

It takes you a few minutes to recover and remove your now soft cock from my pussy filled with semen. You look down at your handiwork and see your sperm coming out of my pussy and the welts you left on my ass and legs. You think maybe you went too far this time, because these wounds are slow to heal.

This concern doesn't last too long and you tell me that if my body would only carry your child, you wouldn't have to fuck me so much. That once my belly starts to swell and my breasts fill with milk, you probably wouldn't have to use the belt and whip to get hard anymore.

You spend some time catching up on work, but you won't let me take a shower because you think you might give me a charge before you have to leave. You tell me to get between your legs and make you hard again.

Since you are still not quite hard and time is running out, I tell you to do whatever you need to do to get there.

You pull me up by my hair and hit me hard in the face out of frustration, the sound of the slap and the shock in my face seem to excite you. Four more times you bring your hand back and the slaps sound. This has had the desired effect on you and you throw me on the bed.

You hold my legs against your shoulders and kick me, push your now hard cock into my wet pussy ... My stocking-clad legs are pushed further back while you try to fuck your cock even deeper into me ... You squeeze the soles of my feet together and work on getting my feet almost completely behind my head ...

Almost completely bent in half, you have full control over my body and I feel you coming closer as you start to move faster. You start to give me some really dirty names and suddenly you punch me in the face for more time and tell me to tell you what you need to hear. I'm asking you to stick your semen inside me, fuck a baby in my stomach.

When you come closer, you put a hand around my neck and start pressing while your orgasm builds up. I feel you start to let go inside me while you call me a dirty cunt and your baby factory. Your hand tightens at my throat as you shoot into me and I get reckless and start to see stars. Finally you stop humming inside me and let your hand out of my throat.

Finally you pull your cock out of my pussy and hold my legs up to make sure your sperm stays in it. You tell me you're not sure what else you can do to put a baby inside me, but you emptied everything you have into me.

You take a shower to get back to your office... You come back into the room in a towel, staring at my body, and even though you have nothing left, you still want to fuck me.

You take out your phone and start taking some photos and videos and move my body into the positions that show your cum inside me or the marks you left on my body.

You grab my chin and kiss me passionately and deeply while your hand gently caresses my belly, hoping that this time it finally worked.

FUCKING THE FIANCÉE

It was well after midnight, and Leo was in a great mood. It was the first night of an amazing festival, and he had stayed out late to watch the last set. Now he wandered back to his tent and the rest of his friends in tears, slightly confused by the flag system, but sure that he would arrive eventually.

As he stopped to fill his bottle from the petrol pump, a small, incredibly drunk guy staggered towards him.

"Yoodude, whatsupp!! He slipped, his arm drifted up and hit his fist.

'Hey man', Leo replied. "I'm a bit lost!

'Ohh, that's, uh,' the guy opened his mouth unsteadily and staggered to the ground. Reflexively, Leo caught him before he struck. Then the guy threw up. Most of it missed, but some of it dripped onto the guy's shirt.

Damn it, Leo thought.

"Sorry, sorry," mumbled the drunk.

"Come on, man, where are you? I'll get you back', Leo said resignedly. He wasn't the most caring, but leaving this guy lying in barf just didn't sit right.

After a few minutes of slow stumbling they reached one of the smaller tents. The man had fallen into a kind of dizziness, but when he saw that the tent brought some energy, he came back to himself.

Katie, hey! Katie!," he groaned as he crawled unsuccessfully for the zipper of the tent. There was a pause, and it was reversed from the inside out.

Ricky', cried a girl from inside. The tent flap fell away, and Leo caught a glimpse of pale arms reaching for the drunk, presumably Ricky. "Shit, what the hell," she exclaimed and smelled the vomit.

'It's okay, I just need sleep, it's okay,' mumbled Ricky, pushed himself past her and collapsed on the tent floor. Leo crouched down to the entrance.

"Hello," he shouted, "I am Leo. I am Leo. I accompanied him from the pump. Ricky waved one arm in Leo's direction.

He saved me, babe, we owe him.

'Oh! Thanks,' said Katie, giving him a quick smile before turning back to Ricky. Leo got an impression of big, innocent eyes and friendly features the second she faced him. It was hard to look at her properly in this light, but she seemed to be petite. Katie bent over to knock Ricky down and Leo caught a glimpse of a perfect peach-colored butt.

'Hey, let me help you,' said Leo and crawled into the tent. Together, they laid Ricky on the front and put a bowl under his mouth. Almost as soon as they sat down, Ricky started snoring.

Any excuse,' Katie said with a sinister look.

Happens a lot, doesn't it?

Every other week, always the same. "The way he grew up," Katie flicked angrily at a mud wrench. He said he'd change once we got married, but who knows when that will be.

"Wow, you are...

-Committed, yeah. Katie reached out a hand, the glimmer of a ring just visible. "He's wonderfully sober, but that's just...

"Too much?" Leo offered.

"Too much?" offered Leo. There was a brief pause. "So, are you camping around here?" Katie said.

'I have no idea,' Leo replied laughing. Red Zone, wherever that is.

'Oh shit', Katie replied, moving away from him and opening a map. 'Yes, it's about an hour's walk from here'.

'Seriously?' replied Katie. Leo looked over at the map. He had been walking in the opposite direction since the set was over.

"Urgh. He raised his hands in desperation.

'Oh, sorry,' said Katie and gave him a quick hug. You did a good thing tonight, fate will make it up to you. Leo felt her breasts pressing against him. As they parted, he carefully weighed his words.

I'm really tired and don't want to go back. So can I sleep here tonight?

"Uh..." he could feel that Katie was torn. Sure, why not? I guess we owe you one,' she said and showed him another smile.

She closed the tent and made room for him on the mattress by wrapping her sleeping bag around her. They lay there for a minute before Leo mentioned the obvious and asked her to share it with him. It was only a small sleeping bag, so they were squeezed together at the end, her hair in his face and her bottom against his crotch.

Time dragged on, and it was clear that neither of them were asleep. Leo turned the situation in his head and made his move. An arm around her stomach, ready to be pulled away when she said something. Not a word. He moved his hand to her chest, gently grabbed a handful and let it slide free. He felt her ass bump against him and she sighed.

They continued as it felt, forever, the question and the answer were obvious to both. One hand gradually became two and her top fell off. Katie had been rubbing against his erection the whole time, and when Leo's hand finally passed her panties, he noticed it was dripping.

His fingers slipped in gently, and the slightest caress of her clitoris left her breathless. Leo teased both her clitoris and her pussy, brought her close to orgasm and disappeared just before. He wanted her to be as horny as he could make her.

At the climax of a near orgasm, he pulled his pants down to her knees and maneuvered his cock between her legs. He slid up behind her and enjoyed the wetness of her cheating pussy.

Suddenly her hand grabbed his head and pulled him towards her. She kissed him hard on the cheek and whispered in his ear.

"I want you to cum inside me.

Leo fucked her slowly, with a little more force at the end of each stroke. It was for her, but also to prolong it. It was a raw thrill to fuck someone's fiancee while she was passed out next to you. It took everything he had not to fill her up right away.

He played for time, changed his position and rolled her over. Every stroke pushed her into the mattress. Out of an impulse, he wiggled his hand under her and reached for her chest, pressing her almost painfully.

His thrusts became fast but steady and he squeezed again. Katie gasped in time and Leo felt her pussy cramping up. He managed one more push, then a hard one came. His balls pumped to the rhythm of her pussy as he flowed in towards her. Both had tried hard to come quietly and it seemed to be enough. Ricky's snoring continued.

As they put their clothes back on, Leo smiled at the thought of his sperm warm inside her. Then he saw Katie leaning over Ricky and whispering something to his sleeping body. Leo thought Ricky was awake for a second, but he was definitely asleep. That's weird.

"What was that?" he whispered. Katie turned to Leo, and her face was surprisingly serious.

I said, "This is for you.

For the rest of the festival, they were a group. Katie was friendly but never flirted while Ricky was awake, picking up one load after another of Leo's sperm as Ricky fainted.

After each night, she whispered the same thing to Ricky, "This is for you.

Three months after the festival, Leo was surprised and happy to be invited to their wedding. It seemed as if something had pushed Ricky to turn the corner. Leo thought of his sperm seeping out of Katie on the last night of the festival and smiled as he clicked on "Present".

THE CABIN

I know how I got here; I just don't know what to do about it. Many of you will think I am a disgusting bitch who doesn't care about herself or others, and to tell you the truth, you are right. If you'd met me two years ago, you'd think I was a prude. You'd never believe that I've had sex with more than 10 different men in the last month. I don't even know most of their names. Still, I crave it. That's how it all started.

To tell you a little bit about me: I'm a small, fit redhead blessed (or sometimes cursed) with firm D-cup breasts. You tend to pay a lot of attention to me. At the same time I often wear clothes that play down their importance. I am a very active person, my husband calls me the Energizer Bunny. I do not go out often and we tend not to talk. Our circle of close friends is small. I work in the financial sector. My job is very demanding and stressful, but I am very well compensated. I guess other people would describe me as classy but friendly. Only recently I have developed a preference for quickies. My husband is more than willing to help me whenever I want. I had started to masturbate, sometimes with toys, when he was away on business.

We have two grown boys who don't live with us. One is in college, the other is working in the world of work. My husband is a good-looking man with a great job. We have a big house in the country. We love camping, going to concerts and doing all the normal things that people do.

There's one thing most people would never believe about me. I love sex, with strangers, outside. How I got to be like this is a pretty long story. Some people like the details, some people don't. I'm the former. This story will be detailed and you will understand how I felt at every step of this experience.

As I said before, I am active. I love a good run in the morning and often find myself hiking or kayaking, anything that takes me outside and into nature. I have always been like this. Last year, during my lunch break from work, I did some hiking on trails that are about 5 minutes away from my work by car. It is a kind of nature reserve, no vehicles are allowed. I drive there, put on my hiking boots and go for a little hike. The parking lot is not very big and there are rarely other cars there. Sometimes, when my husband is away on business, I drive there in the evening. We live in a small town and it is very safe.

The road system is quite complicated. In winter it is used as a cross-country skiing track, and in summer people go by bike, walk their dogs and hike there. The tracks have a fairly large outer loop, with quite a lot of forks and inner loops. I had taken the same route because I need just enough time to get around during my lunch break. On one occasion, last year, I decided to take another fork and follow one of the inner loops. I came across a small clearing and found a hut that is obviously used by skiers in winter. I got curious and went inside.

What I saw in the hut shocked me at first. There were indications that people had sex there. I found used condoms, wrappers etc. and even a pair of ladies' panties. At first I was quite disgusted and left. I thought, "What kind of slut would have sex in there and leave her panties behind? The next few days I started thinking about who would have sex in there. It seemed to me that it would most likely be people, probably married people, who would go there to cheat on their spouses. I told one of my long-time girlfriends what I had found in the woods and she told me that she and her current boyfriend were out there "grim". I'm not very familiar with the deviant sex vocabulary, so I had to get her to explain what she meant. Most of you know what it means, but she told me that her boyfriend loved going out into the woods with her and having sex there, sometimes in front of other people. I had no idea that was "a thing." I just couldn't figure out what kind of payoff it was for her, but she said it was very exciting and they didn't do it often.

In the following weeks I still hiked there, but avoided the hut. Apart from that I am a very curious woman and the train to the hut was always present. Every time I hiked, I found myself thinking about going back to the hut, not knowing exactly why, but it definitely occurred to me. I remember having the opportunity for an early lunch on a Wednesday and deciding to hike again. When I arrived at the parking lot, I noticed a very shiny new Lexus parked there. I ventured down the path. When I reached the fork in the road leading to the hut, the bait was too big; my curiosity forced me to do so. When I approached it, it seemed deserted. When I entered, I was shocked, repulsed and yet petrified. There was a middle-aged man, tall, obese, well-dressed. His fly was open and he was masturbating. I froze. Every fibre in my being told me to get out, but I couldn't move. He didn't stop, he just smiled at me and went on.

I still remember his look and his cock. He was focused on what he was doing, beads of sweat on his forehead. His cock was thick and long. His fleshy hands wrapped around it as he pumped it. He muttered a few words and persuaded me to "help". I shook my head negatively, but stayed there, feet away from him. He said something like, "Suit yourself, I don't mind if you watch." He went on for a few moments and then emitted a deep groan as huge streams of semen erupted from him. They flew so far that I had to lift my foot so he wouldn't splash it. He silently closed the zipper and slid past me on his way out. I was still in shock when I looked at his sperm on the floor. I couldn't believe how much it was.

When I came out of my stupor, I realized where I was and I was afraid of getting caught. I rushed out of the booth and back to my car. I returned to work and had 20 minutes left for lunch. Once there, I had calmed down sufficiently and realized that I was highly excited. I was so wet that I was afraid that employees and customers might recognize my state of arousal, so I made a decision as a manager. I went down the stairs to the floor below my office, found the handicapped washroom, went inside, locked the door and masturbated until orgasm. I came so hard that I was surprised that nobody heard me. Not only did I rub myself, but I put several fingers inside me and squirted quite a lot, so much that I had to clean the toilet I was sitting on.

I went back to my office and was quite ashamed, but I could NOT get the image of him masturbating out of my head. Luckily my husband was away on business, so I didn't have to worry about him feeling anything else about me. After work I got into my car. It was like a dream, I was in a haze, and when I came to, I realized that I was in the parking lot of the hiking trails. I was trembling, excited and felt a little sick. Nevertheless, I got out of the car and walked down the paths towards the hut. To this day I don't know what I expected, but I found myself in the hut, sitting on the bench with my fingers in my pussy. I came, hard, and made up my panties and skirt. When I calmed down, I left the cabin. When I arrived at the beginning of the path, I saw a young couple with a blanket under their arms entering the path. I was horrified that they could see the wet stains on my skirt.

I got into my car and drove home. I was confused and frightened. I wondered what would have happened if I had been caught there. I fell asleep. The next morning I woke up and got ready for work. I thought about what kind of clothes I would have to wear to reduce the risk of my clothes being smeared with LOL. The only thing I could think of was to take a towel or blanket and when I went back, take off my underpants/panties and put them back on again. It was as if my subconscious had taken over, and when I wanted to leave I threw a small towel in the back of the car. When I got to work, I got my laptop and lunch from the back seat. I saw the towel I had put there and felt a little shame and disgust, but I quickly let that go out of my head.

This morning at work was LONG. I was restless and fidgety. I tried not to think about the cabin, but it kept popping into my mind. At lunch it was as if I was on autopilot. I found myself back in the cabin, naked from the waist down, sitting on my towel and fingered myself like crazy to get out as quickly as possible. Every little rustle that the wind made scared me, but finally I reached orgasm and hurried back to work. This routine lasted for several weeks until one day I was near my orgasm and a dog stuck his head in the cabin. I didn't hear him approaching and that really scared me. He didn't come into the cabin, his owner, a male dog, called him over and he ran away. My orgasm hit so violently that I literally splashed across the whole width of the room. I was so startled that I did not go back into the cabin for a few weeks.

In those few weeks my head was buzzing. Every time I was alone, I masturbated thinking about what would have happened if I had been caught. I had no preconceived ideas about what I would do, only the image of a stranger coming in the doorway while I was in the middle of orgasm made me cum hard. I squirted a lot and had masturbated on the floor of the washroom or in the bathtub to make it easier to clean up afterwards.

When I finally had the courage to return to the cabin, the season was almost over. I went there almost daily until it got too cold. It took longer and longer until I reached orgasm. I am now convinced that I deliberately slowed down to increase the chance that someone else would come in with me. That winter, I even convinced my husband to start cross-country skiing. We went to the hut a few times and even had a quickie there. The hut had been cleaned up by the skiers, the graffiti had been painted over and the floors had been well cleaned. Someone even installed a small wood stove on a big brick block outside, and more than once we found the hut to warm up.

Spring could not have come earlier for me. I seemed too anxious to return to the hut. The first hike did not go well. It was wet and muddy, and I turned back before I got there. I waited another week and masturbated at every opportunity. When I got back, it was dry enough to make it there. I masturbated slowly; I barely made it back to work in time. This routine continued for about a week. I still remember the day the routine changed. It was a Thursday, I had masturbated there at noon, and since my husband was not there, I went back in the evening. I got out of my car, grabbed my towel and headed for the hiking trail. When I entered the path, I looked back and saw another car entering the parking lot. A man got out. My heart was racing. He was alone. I noticed he was tall and thin, but I couldn't see him clearly. He definitely saw me, and as I walked along the path, he followed me, but kept his distance. I was wearing yoga pants, a tank top and a sweater.

When I came to the fork in the path leading to the cabin, my mind screamed that I should swerve, but my body had other ideas. I walked along the path. When I got to the cabin, I didn't know if he was still following me. I sat down on the bench and waited. My heart was racing. I didn't dare touch myself, although I was overexcited. In fact, I could hear him approaching. He stopped before he entered. I was paralyzed with fear. I was breathing very heavily. When he finally entered the cabin, he was about three feet in front of me. We didn't say anything, just stared at each other. Finally, I took the strength to ask him, "What do you want?" He answered, "I don't know," and he walked a few steps towards me. He was wearing nylon running trousers, including a sweatshirt and a muscle shirt. I looked at him, and he adjusted his stride. To this day I don't know what got into me, but I reached out my hand and felt his step. He was semi-erect and wasn't wearing any underpants.

Again it was like a dream. I stroked him a few times, then I rolled my fingers under the elastic waistband and pulled on him. His cock jumped free and then he was in my mouth. I sucked it eagerly. It wasn't huge, I had no problem taking the whole length. When he was about to cum, I thought about what I wanted to do, take him out and jerk him off? No, too risky, he might jerk off on me. He tried to pull away, but I held him there as his sperm shot out of his cock. I swallowed it. I remember thinking it wasn't as bad as I thought it was gonna be, swallowing. It tasted salty, earthy. When he pulled away from me, he pulled up his pants in silence and left. No thanks, it was good or something. He just walked away. I sat there, vibrating, ashamed and at the same time extremely aroused. I thought about leaving, but I didn't want to run into him again on the paths. I decided to drop myself off.

I took off my yoga pants and sat down on the bench again. It felt cold, but I started to touch myself. The mixed emotions stirred up my desire and soon I was completely gone. I realized that I was not determined to have a quick orgasm. I played with my lips and clitoris and enjoyed the sensations. Then I heard another sound. I froze. It sounded as if someone was approaching again. I sat there, half-naked on the bench, legs spread, hand on my sex, and my mind was moving at a million miles a minute. It felt like an eternity. I tormented myself putting my pants back on, but for some reason I didn't. When he entered the cabin, I immediately recognized him as the man I had walked into the season before. He smiled confidently and without a word, pulled his cock out. Before I knew it, I had his thick flesh in my hand and was stroking him. All I could think of was: "Holy shit, what am I doing, I just cheated on my husband with a complete stranger and now it's going to happen again".

I put it in my mouth. It tasted like sweat, very revolting, but I kept sucking. It erected in my mouth and it was too much for me. I gagged him, mainly because of the size, but partly also because of the smell. I felt sick to my stomach, but I kept on sucking. I just wanted to get rid of him and get out of there. He had other ideas. He seemed a little frustrated with my attempts to stick him in the throat. I gagged a lot. Eventually, he pulled it out of my mouth. He raised his hand in front of me and took out a condom. Almost robotically I took it off him, opened it and pushed it on him. He lifted me into a standing position and then told me to turn around. I hesitated and he took my elbow and led me. He is a whole lot bigger than me, so I knelt down on the bench voluntarily and I felt him touching my pussy. It was like electricity shooting through me. He pushed it against my hole. He adjusted my position and pushed it into me. My body literally exploded in orgasm.

He fucked me hard, holding me up with one arm around my waist. It was animalistic, and I was having orgasms all the time. He fucked me like a dog in heat. I could see he was about to orgasm, but he pulled the condom out and took it off. I was terribly afraid that he had put it back in me, but again he led me and turned me around and put the condom back in my face, twitching. Before I could react, he erupted in my face. His sperm was hot and thick and some of it ended up in my mouth, most of it was on my face and some of it ended up on my shirt and sweater. I realized that I was on my knees in front of him. I grabbed my towel and tried to clean up. At that point the light was very dim. He said a few words to me; I could not say which ones they were.

He closed the zipper and left. I sat down on the bench again and sobbed. Not only had I been very sloppy, but it was the first time I had cheated on my husband with two differ-ent men. I did not know their names. I cleaned up as much as I could. I put on my pants, but by then it was already dark. I left the cabin, and only when I came home did I realize that I had left my pants there. Now I was the bitch who fucks in the cabin.

14 stories: The JIXX Book of Hidden Pleasure

The Best Way to Spend Good Time with Your Playmate

Rose Reed

Table of Contents

NOT A CHEATER

I love my fiancé. I really love him. I never thought of myself as the cheating type. I had always been a loyal relationship person.

These were the thoughts that ran through my head when I saw this gorgeous little brunette bomb, who was definitely not my fiancé, bouncing enthusiastically on my cock. I thought of my fiancé as this beauty repeatedly impaled herself on my cock and screamed as her tiny cunt stretched out to meet me halfway.

No, I wasn't the cheating type.

But there I was, my aching balls buried up to my eyeballs in a girl I had only met a few moments earlier. There I was, trying desperately not to explode in her too soon. I needed that to hold out. If I had put myself in this situation, well, fuck it... I had to make it worth my while!

We had met that night on the beach. I had been surfing that night, and when I went back to my car, I found her leaning against my car. My cock wiggled at the sight of these pretty brunettes wearing tiny jeans shorts and a see-through white lace top, leaning casually against my ute. She spoke to me, but I was distracted by her taut legs, curvy waist and pouting lips. Lips that wrapped perfectly around my...

"And?" Her singing voice cut through my forbidden thoughts.

"Well, what?" I asked silently. My face felt red. I softly urged my dick to behave.

"Uh... "I just told you that my car broke down... I asked you to give me a ride into town. So...?"

I nodded a bit too enthusiastically. She smiled and spread her crossed arms.

She was even more beautiful when she smiled.

"Thank you very much. "I can't tell you how much of a relief it is. I thought I was stuck here, then I saw your ute. I thought I'd just wait here until the owner came back and hitchhike back to town."

I just nodded, mute.

I told her to wait while I changed. I made my way to the shower block and turned on the outdoor shower. While I was showering, I turned around and looked at the girl who was waiting for me, evil thoughts were running through my head. Thoughts that mainly consisted of this girl sipping naked on my cock, taking it from behind, riding me...

Shit, man. I'm a happily married man. Sex with my fiancé may be rare lately, very rare, but that was no reason for me to get lost!

We drove to her house. We made small talk the whole way there. She invited me in. And I followed her, like an obedient puppy. She offered me a beer. I took it. She asked me to come to her bedroom. I followed her, only too willingly.

And then it happened. The moment you have the chance - your last chance - to withdraw before you get into a situation you know is almost impossible to leave. The moment when, once it's over, you're too far away...

I won't lie, when she slipped out of her shorts and got down on her knees, I had completely forgotten my fiancé. I couldn't get her out of my mind when my little beach girl pulled my cock out of my underpants and blew me with such enthusiasm.

I was a bad, terrible, shameful man. I stood there without a single word or sound of protest as this ravishing stranger greedily slurped my cock.

I almost came to my senses. For a very brief moment. And then the now naked beauty spread herself on me and filled her incredibly tight cunt with my cock. And then she jumped on me, fucked me, rubbed her clitoris against me, screamed...

I had my hands on her hips and I led her. I led her up and down on my engaged cock, desperately trying to empty my load into her. I cared about nothing more than my cock and her sweet, tiny cunt. Nothing else mattered. No one else.

She came at me fiercely. Her cunt started to spasm. It felt like she was milking me, her muscles pressing down furiously and hard. I was at my peak too, my charge was pumping deep into her. She bucked and arched her back. Her perfect tits, her little body covered in sweat... she was so fucking delicious!

We both came in hard. She swore repeatedly, her whole body trembled as she pressed her palms into my chest to calm down. I wanted to scream with pleasure, but instead I let out a deep, deep growl.

She climbed off my softening cock and kissed me gently. It was our first kiss. And I knew it would be our last. I got dressed and left quickly. I started to drive home, a mixture of feelings. Partly strong feelings of guilt. Some of them insanely happy.

I'd just cheated. I was a cheat. It felt so phony and dirty, and I knew deep down I would never stray from the path again. But I also had the sweet, satisfying memory of the sexiest, sluttiest girl I had ever met, and her beautiful face when she came violently on my cock.

A WEDDING QUICKIE

I don't understand people who don't like weddings, I love them. Drinks, food, brides-maids, what's not to like? When my friend Jennifer got married, I looked forward to it until I realized how stressed out everyone was. My girlfriend was the maid of honor, and she got way too excited about it. On that day the bridal party was not very well or-ganized, so I was leashed to help out, bring bags to the hotel and stuff like that. The wedding was fine, but when we arrived at the hotel, Jennifer wanted a ridiculous num-ber of official photos on the grounds showing her and her new husband in different pos-es. I think even the photographer was bored, and he got paid for it.

While they were being photographed and my friend was supervising, I met Jennifer's older sister Cara. I knew the family since we were kids and even dated Cara briefly when we were younger, but she was married now and we didn't see each other as often as we would have liked. In her bridesmaid's dress she looked damn hot though, it was a long, dark purple dress, but it was skintight and had a corset-style waist. She had her dark blonde hair professionally curled and tied together, with a few curls hanging down to frame her face.

We were young when we dated, and she had always maintained that she didn't want to have sex until she was married. She always let me finger her while she jerked me off, but we never had sex. But now that she was married, I think she somehow realized that sex isn't necessarily as big a deal as some people make it out to be. Although she was a ra-ther shy and reserved woman by nature, she was more open and flirting with me in the last months. Somehow I got the feeling that maybe she regretted not having had a bit more fun when she was young and single.

I politely told her that the bridesmaid dress would suit her and to my slight surprise she told me that I looked really hot in my dark suit. She winked at me as she said this and sneaked a shy sip of her drink through a straw. We continued talking until Cara said, "Oh, that reminds me, I have some of Jennifer's bags in my car, would you please help me take them upstairs?

Of course I didn't mind, so we went outside, got a few bags from the car and I followed Cara to her room. She said we'd just put everything in her room and Jennifer could pick up her stuff later.

The room Cara had booked with her husband was bigger than the one my girlfriend and I had, and when we put the suitcases down, I wondered at the window if they had a view. I don't know why I always do this in hotels, I think it's just a habit. As soon as I turned away from the window, Cara, who had moved in right behind me, quickly went in and pressed her lips against mine. I was shocked, and before I had time to react, she put her arms around my neck and shoved her tongue in my mouth. I didn't know what to do, so I just grabbed her by the waist and kissed her back.

She pressed her body against mine and I ran my hands over her firm ass. When I grabbed it tight, she let out a moan and kissed me harder. I remembered how sensitive her little breasts were, so I raised one hand up, ran it over her chest and grabbed one of them. As I pressed her gently, she pulled her mouth away from mine, moaned loudly and said, "I need you, I want it right now, I need you inside me.

Desperately she began to pull up the long thick hem of her dress and bundle it in her arms.

"Are you sure about this?" I asked and immediately regretted this question.

"Yes, I need it," she moaned.

When she managed to get most of her dress over her hips, she looked down and said, "The damn corset is so tight that I'm going to bend down, you can fuck me from behind. I couldn't believe what was happening, I had never seen her act like that before. Actually, come to think of it, I don't think I had ever heard her curse before.

I hadn't even finished that thought before she turned around and bent over the bed, still clutching her dress. I looked down to see her amazingly sexy bottom in tight black panties. Her long smooth legs stood straight and slightly spread.

I quickly pulled down my zipper and pulled my cock out as I got up behind her and her panties slipped down her legs. I ran the head of my cock over the lips of her pussy and found that she was soaking wet. I rubbed it up and down her lips a couple of times and she moaned, "Stick it in me, please fuck me".

She was so wet that when I lined her up and pushed her forward, my cock was sunk about halfway into her pussy. We both grunted loudly, and I pulled back a little and pushed myself forward again. I could not believe that I finally fucked so horny, her warm pussy was the tightest I had ever felt. I started banging back and forth and soon I was completely buried in her.

After a minute or two she stabilized on one elbow and reached back to rub with one hand while I fucked her. I had no idea why she was so horny, but she was really keen on it, she pushed her hips back to meet mine and grunted with every thrust.

"Oh fuck," she moaned, "she's so big, you're so much bigger than Dom."

It hadn't hit me until then, I knew she was a virgin when she got married, and as far as I knew, she had only ever had sex with her husband. I kept hitting her, and it wasn't long before her moans became louder and her rubbing more hectic.

I hit her as hard as I could while she was grinding her teeth and her tight pussy got even tighter around my cock when she came. I slowed down a bit as she came down from her orgasm and then continued stomping again until I felt I was coming too.

I moaned, "Damn, this tight pussy's gonna make me cum." I moaned, "Where do you want it?"

"Not on the dress," she almost screamed, "please, not on the dress."

She thought for a second and then said, "Um, just do it inside me."

I didn't need to be told twice, I stabbed myself a few more times, buried myself deep, grunted, and exploded a load of cum inside Cara's pussy. After taking a breath for a minute I pulled my cock out and she immediately put one hand down and cupped it over her pussy. A bit awkwardly she stood up, reached down with her other hand and pulled her panties up so that nothing of my sperm could escape.

With a smile she kissed me on the lips and said: "That was incredible, but I have to clean up before I ruin this dress, see you downstairs?

"Sure," I replied as I watched her shuffle into the bathroom to wash my sperm out of her. I wiped my cock with a few cloths from the dresser and stuffed it back into my pants before letting myself out. When I got back to the bar, my phone beeped with a text message from Cara. It said, "Thanks for that, your dick felt great. Maybe later we can see how much of it fits in my mouth?

BEACH HOUSE

After what happened on my PS4 night, I was hoping that Chris would not push his luck with Zoe from now on. They haven't seen each other since, but we see him on weekends with other friends.

Zoe and I had planned to go to her parents' beach house this weekend, but our friends somehow also invited themselves to a big drinking and sunbathing session. Zoe couldn't say no to them after they got too excited about it. She's too nice sometimes. But that will not stop us from enjoying it anyway, we love the company of our friends.

Actually, it was Zoe's best friend Sarah who invited herself along with her boyfriend Greg. I'd only met Greg twice at parties and didn't really get along with him. He's a gym buff like Zoe. I'm pretty sure he's on steroids for the size of his muscles, but he claims it's just his hard work. He's humiliating and arrogant sometimes. With Zoe, he's actually quite grasping, he palpates easily from time to time, even in front of me, a guy he just met. Sarah didn't seem to mind, though. Sarah is quite similar to Zoe in personality, she is about 1.70 m tall, petite, blond and we get along well. After Sarah had secured her invitation, Zoe told me to invite the boys as well. Steve and Chris were the only two who could make it.

Zoe and I took Chris and Steve to the house in our car. We planned to get there before Sarah and Greg, so we could unlock the house and get everything up and running. On the drive there, Chris told us all that he could hardly wait to go swimming. Then he made a remark about how he couldn't wait to see Zoe's butt in his bikini too. Chris then told Steve everything that happened after Steve left on my PS4 night. Steve called it bullshit, but Zoe actually confirmed quickly that it did happen.

Steve has been my best friend since I was a kid and has never been rude or flirtatious with my girlfriends, he has always been very respectful. This time, however, he gave Chris a high five five and just said it nicely. Since Steve is without his wife on this trip, he may just be bringing forth a new Steve with fewer boundaries. His wife wasn't too bad, to be fair, but she kept him on a short leash at parties and so on. He was just lucky that she could not become unemployed for the trip and decided to stay at home with her children.

Chris then started bugging Zoe about what kind of bikini she'd taken. Zoe just rolled her eyes and laughed. She said he just had to wait and see. Chris whined and played like a child who's not fair.

We got to the house and dumped our bags in our rooms. There were only two bedrooms, both with double beds. We obviously claimed the master bedroom. Chris and Steve wanted to sleep on the pull-out sofa bed in the living room. This meant that Sarah and Greg would have privacy in their own room. Chris and Steve both claimed that they were too drunk to take care of the sleeping arrangements anyway.

Sarah and Greg arrived about an hour later. Zoe showed them their room and led them up to the back deck where I and the boys were. I introduced her friends to mine, and then we all sat in the loungers, drinking and enjoying the sun. Chris came to the fridge after a beer and took out his swimming trunks when he asked if anyone else wanted to take a bath. We all agreed and went inside to put on our bathing suits. Zoe was wearing a sexy black bikini with pants cut higher than a normal bikini but not really a thong.

We all met back out on deck and Chris Wolf whistled at Zoe. Zoe just slapped his arm and laughed. Greg then supported Chris' approval of her clothes and slapped her on the butt, making her wobble. Everyone laughed about it and continued drinking. Sarah wore a modest red bikini but still showed her hot body.

Chris, Greg and Zoe went swimming in the ocean while I was getting the grill going. Steve was talking to Sarah and they were both flirting a bit. I looked out at the sea and watched them splashing each other and having fun. A few minutes later they came back into the house. Chris and Greg laughed and Zoe had a grin on her face and playfully slapped them both. I asked what that was about. She told us that a big wave had just knocked her bikini top to the side and they were getting to see the breasts. Then she told them that they were like children who had seen their first tit. They both laughed and asked to see the other one. We all laughed about it until Zoe quickly showed us all her breasts and said that there were enough breasts for now to cover them again. All Sarah said to Greg was to leave the poor girl alone. Then we all calmed down and had dinner.

Not much else happened that night, we all went to bed without incident. That was until Zoe got up in the middle of the night to get a glass of water. I saw her get up and go to the door, just in her baggy shirt with no bra and her black thong. The shirt didn't cover much of her bottom, I could see her thong clearly. I asked her quietly if she would put something on. She said that she hadn't packed her bathrobe and that the boys would sleep in the living room anyway. Then she left.

I fell asleep again for about 30 minutes and noticed that she was still gone. I looked in the living room and couldn't see her. Steve was fast asleep on the sofa bed, but Chris had disappeared. I looked outside and saw that the deck light was on behind the curtain. I peeked behind the curtain, looked through the screen door and saw Zoe, Chris and Greg all talking. Zoe didn't come back to change, so the boys got a look. To be fair to Zoe, she had her water while the boys drank beer. She got up and announced she was going back to bed. Chris asked if he could come, too. Zoe replied, not tonight, I need sleep. Greg whispered something to Chris, then Chris forced Zoe quickly and held her over the table, she seemed too tired and hungover to resist, so she just let him. Greg pulled her shirt over her back and felt her bottom over her thong. Greg asked her if anyone had ever spanked her. Zoe replied that she actually manages to get spanked quite often. Greg slapped her hard on the butt, causing her to cry out. He said with a butt like that, he could believe it. Then Zoe got up, rubbed her bottom and tired eyes and then said she'd see her in the morning. Greg stood in front of her and said she could only go to bed if he kissed her good night. Zoe said okay, but just a little one. Greg started to kiss her and grabbed the back of her head, I could see their tongues wiggling together. Greg's hands went to her ass, and then she pushed away, said good night and started to come in. I went to bed quickly so I wouldn't get caught spying.

She went to bed, reached over and grabbed my semi-hard dick. She got under the sheets and lay on top of me. She really wanted to try it. Then she stopped, took off all her clothes and started riding me as a reverse cowgirl. I love this position, I can see her perfect ass rubbing up against me. I notice Greg's handprint on her ass. I decided to tease her with it. I asked her whose handprint that was while squeezing her ass cheeks. She moans and admits that it's Greg's handprint. I asked her if she was naughty, if you deserved it. She just moaned that she always deserved a spanking because she's always naughty. I reached for her clit and I rubbed it and we both came at it hard. We both calmed down and went back to sleep.

When I woke up, I saw that Zoe was already gone. I went into the living room and most of them were having breakfast, Zoe wasn't there, but I heard the shower running. I poured myself an orange juice and heard someone coming out of the bathroom. I turned around and saw Chris coming out. But the shower was still running, and everybody else was there except Zoe. Chris said he would never drink that much again. I suspected he'd just been sick. I heard the shower being turned off and Zoe came out in a towel. She said good morning and went into the bedroom.

I followed her and asked her if she knew Chris was in there. She laughed and said, "Yeah, it was disgusting. I asked her if he saw anything behind the curtain. She smiled and said he might have seen something. She's such a pain in the ass. She said she felt sorry for him, so she gave him a quick flash to cheer him up. I asked him what he saw. She said "full frontal" in her sweet, sexy voice and then she dropped her towel. She is gorgeous, she walked slowly towards me, stroking her breasts and then down to her shaved pussy, then she whispered, he saw all this. Then she giggled and then got ready. My dick hurt.

During the day we sunbathed, swam, drank, ate and drank some more. Zoe flirted with the boys all day and kept them on the go. Sarah also flirted her part of the flirt. After the sun went down, we were all drunk. Steve sleeps in mine and Zoe's bed, he was so drunk that he bathed himself naked and started waving his cock around in front of the girls. Me and Zoe let him use the bed for a while so he could sleep it off. Greg and Sarah had too much, too, so they retired for the night. Then I fell asleep in a chair, too, leaving Chris and Zoe alone.

I woke up a few hours later. Chris slept in his pull-out sofa bed, but next to him under the sheets was Zoe. She looked naked, but I couldn't see for sure. I went over and shook her awake. She looked up at me and seemed confused because she was in bed with another man. I asked her what had happened. She rubbed her eyes and the sheet fell off her and revealed her topless. She told me not to be angry, she said she was and still was su-per drunk. She said that they had set up the bed and decided to sleep there that night. She said it was all harmless and she wanted to go straight to sleep but she felt Chris rub-bing his naked cock against her ass. She said she got too excited and they started making out. Chris undressed her and then she took them off. She told him to keep her thong on. She pulled the sheet back to show me that she still had her thongs on. She went on about what had happened and said one thing led to another and she blew him. Then she said that's all that happened. Later I got her to admit that she had swallowed his sperm, too.

We both sat on the terrace to collect our thoughts. She kept saying she was sorry, but I wasn't really mad. My dick was rock hard. Zoe noticed that and smiled. She grabbed my cock and said, "I suppose you forgive me now. Then she went on to let me cum in her mouth.

I didn't let Chris see that I knew what had happened and told Zoe to forget it. She told me that she was grateful that I was understanding and that she loved me. This away weekend was just what we needed, and I must say I think everyone else enjoyed it, too.

A GROPE IN THE DARK

My husband Roger and I were driving through Wyoming when we were trapped by a huge ice storm. I-80 was completely closed in both directions when highway patrol turned everyone off the highway. It was the Saturday after Thanksgiving, and the road was jammed. All available motel rooms were filled within a very short time. We were taken in by a nice Mormon family who fed us - apparently they always have a supply of food available for emergencies - and were allowed to sleep on the floor in the basement because all the beds were occupied. Five of us slept in the same room in loose bed rolls made of blankets. When the lights went out, it was pitch black except for a night light coming from the bathroom at the end of the hall.

I don't know how long I slept, but I was awakened by a movement. I was lying on my left side looking at the back of my sleeping man, and the man on the other side was gently stroking my hand. Had he not been so gentle, had he been persistent or demanding, I might have knocked him away, but that happened very gently and kindly.

In a fog I thought about who was lying next to me. He was a quiet, gentle man, about my age, with attractive eyes and a firm chin. It was not the face of an unkind man or a pervert. I decided to let him continue rubbing my hand. The rubbing turned more into a massage as he kneaded the muscles of my hand and wrist. It felt good and was harmless. I reached out my arm to him, which let him know I was awake and that I did not disapprove. I sighed gently and showed that I enjoyed secretly holding hands. It was a little naughty lying next to my husband and I felt a slight agitation.

As he continued his service there was a slight rustling as he somehow repositioned himself behind my back. He took my hand and positioned it around something warm and hard. It was his penis!

I could have ripped my hand away. I probably should have, but I was fascinated. For ten years I had not felt the penis of any man other than my husband! It felt comfortable, hard and soft at the same time, and silky to the touch. I slowly felt its length up and down. It was tapping in my hand, like a living being. I explored his base and found the man's balls. I rubbed them with my palm and they felt full and soft and non-threatening. I was content to slowly and quietly glide my hand up and down over this man's penis while listening to my husband snoring softly beside me.

"What's the big deal?" I thought. I can do something we'll both remember without taking anything away from my husband. I can make this man happy, give him pleasure and feel a little excitement for myself. The more I thought, while continuing to rub gently, the more determined I became to get rid of this man. That would be fun.

I tightened my grip and started pumping faster. The man joined me with his own hand and adjusted my speed to what he wanted. I did this for a minute, but I did not want to miss the opportunity by hurrying too much. I stopped the pumping and took a moment to feel his balls again. I could tell by his ragged breath that he enjoyed it immensely. I examined the tip and found that a generous amount of prepuce was dripping from it. I felt deliciously naughty, so I rubbed the prepuce on my fingers and put it in my mouth. It tasted warm, creamy and very masculine. I felt a pulse of wetness in my pussy. I freed my left arm, on which I was lying to touch myself, rolled slowly on my back, my right hand holding this strange man's cock and my husband snoring next to me.

It was not my intention, but the man felt that this was an invitation. He rolled closer so that his penis was on my hip on my pajama pants. He put his hand gently on my stomach and pushed it up under my pajama bottoms. He wanted to touch my breasts! I gently took his hand, moved it away and put it on my flat stomach. He could touch me, but not in my private parts. He started to gently rub my belly and it felt good.

I thought back to the events of the day. It had not been a good day for Roger and me. We never should have taken that stupid trip to see his family. It always ended in a fight about politics that nobody ever won. Roger was as stubborn as ever, and in the end we stormed off a day earlier than we planned.

What's this? The man's hand had worked its way back up to my breasts. It lay on the outside and slid gently over one and the other. I felt a slight tingling sensation every time it touched my erect nipples. I'm sure he could feel them. His touch was so beautiful that I allowed him to continue.

I hadn't wanted to make the trip today. I knew the weather forecast. The Wyoming Highway Patrol had a warning on the Internet about travel. I told Roger, but he blew it off, like he always does. If the message came from a woman, she couldn't be that reliable. Son of a bitch.

I realized immediately that while I was distracted by these thoughts, the man's hand had moved up inside my shirt. It felt beautiful. I sighed. If Roger hadn't been such a pig, we'd never have been here. He deserved a little revenge. I decided to let the man continue. I realized I wasn't stroking his dick anymore. He had done nothing about it. What a nice, patient man! I continued stroking him and felt rewarded when he softly hummed his approval.

In the meantime his friendly fingers had begun to pay special attention to my nipples, which were stiff and demanded attention. He whirled his finger around the left one and pressed against it. Then he pinched and pulled it. The sudden wave of pleasure made me gasp. My hips involuntarily wiggled and my pussy got wet. I noticed that I held my breath and emitted a huge sigh.

The man took this as further encouragement and continued to caress my breasts and press my nipples, one after the other. My sigh that sounded like encouragement now became real encouragement. I turned and continued to pump on the man's tail to spur him on. I wanted more. I longed to be touched in a different way.

As I surrendered more and more to my rising lust, I hooked my thumbs into my pajamas at the waist and pulled them down along with my panties. I sat up long enough to pull them up to my ankles and lay down again. As I did so, I pulled my shirt over my bare breasts. "Here," I thought to myself. "Take what you want."

As I felt the cool air flowing over my body, the man's hand went straight into my lower half. He stroked my inner legs with his palm until I could barely stand it. I pulled my heels up to my buttocks and spread my knees wide in a lewd posture. I thought: "There, silly! Here's my pussy! Use it for something!"

He got the message. He pressed a finger inside my wet pussy and slowly began to move his finger in and out of me. It was beautiful! He investigated this way for a while, then pulled his finger out and rubbed it against my clitoris. I jumped. I felt a wave of pleasure rush over my whole body, almost like an orgasm. The man rubbed him again, and a third time. Once more, and I was sure I would come!

But it was not like that. The man resumed his attack with his fingers, this time with two fingers. At first he started slowly and increased his speed. That in itself was tremendously enjoyable. Every time he pressed his fingers in, it was a big "fuck you!" for my husband Roger. "Fuck you, Roger. Your wife gets finger-banged by a stranger while you lie and snore like a pig because you wouldn't take her advice. You'll never know, but I'll always know that you got paid. Paid in full."

I started to absently pinch my own nipples with my free left hand. I turned my attention to the cock in my hand. I began timing my handshake to the beat of the fingers of the man inside of me. He seemed to like that and he pushed his cock closer, encouragingly. Was he imagining that he was inside me? Should my hand be my pussy? He wanted to fuck me! I imagined that his fingers were his cock, deep inside my pussy, and said to Roger "Fuck you!" and to me "I want to come inside you! I imagined that he was actually fucking me with his dick inside me, over and over and over and over and over again...

And what if I let him actually fuck me? If I let him climb up and stick his big fat cock in my pussy. What if Roger woke up? "Hey, Roger. How about this. He fucks me. A stranger is fucking your wife, and she likes it. What's that, Roger? No, I'm not gonna stop. I'm going to keep fucking him until we're both finished! Turn on the light so you can watch. Maybe I'll let someone else do it too!" When I imagined this, my desire began to grow.

I was still lying there on my back with my heels beside my buttocks. We increased our pace. He put the thumb of his hand into action and with every stroke he pushed his thumb against my clitoris. That was finally it. I felt the rise of a huge orgasm. I lifted my pelvis from the floor and pushed my pussy bawdy into the sky. I probably suffered brain damage from not screaming, but I managed not to do it. I must have come three times like that, with my pussy in the air and the fingers of a strange man hitting me in and out. I lay down in a mist of bliss and struggled to catch my breath again.

As I connected with my surroundings, I remembered my stranger. He was still dissatisfied. He certainly deserved to be cared for. I don't know what I expected - that my husband would wake up with sperm on me and my bed roll? The solution was obvious.

I crawled downstairs and put the man's cock in my mouth. I could tell by the panting and control of his breathing that he liked it. I caressed his shaft and stroked his balls. I ran my tongue around the needy tip of his cock and lowered my head on it until I was almost gagged. I began to bob my head rhythmically up and down. The man reached for a handful of my hair, but not in a controlling, rude way. He let me move my head freely at my own pace. Finally, as he tightened, I knew it was coming. He injected a hot dose of fresh sperm into my mouth, which I swallowed immediately. This was followed by another one and another one. I could hardly keep up. Finally it was over and he collapsed, spent.

I lay there and thought. I don't even know the guy's name. I can't even imagine his face. I don't even know if I like him as a person. But I like him as a lover. I don't think there will be a future for us - it was just something that happened one night. What would breakfast look like?

I get up to clean up and wash off the smell of sex. When I got back to my bedroll, the man was gone. Maybe he spent the rest of the night in his truck or on foot, I don't know, but I can imagine he was smiling. I never saw him again. Take this, Roger.

WIFE'S RIDE HOME

About 10 years ago, my wife was attending bunco parties in another neighborhood. If you don't know Bunco, it's a dice game, and as far as I know it's popular with women as a night out, at least in our neighborhood. It's an excuse to get together and have a few drinks, to be honest. At the time my wife was about 42, 5'9", 140lbs, with medium-length brown hair and green eyes. It was the middle of summer and an extremely hot night. My wife was wearing a simple pair of sandals and a short cotton sundress, which she usually wore only as a beach blanket.

Not unlike on other occasions, I dropped my wife off with the plan to either call her or go with one of her friends. The games usually ended around 22:30 or 23:00. Around 10:00 p.m. I received a call from her that she was going to go with her friend Sheila.

I always wait for my wife when she was on the road and was expecting her around 11 pm. I was a bit shocked but not overly concerned when she came home around 12:30. Our garage has two cars under the basement, which means that when I look out of the family room I look down on our driveway, which slopes down to the street. When my wife came home, I heard the car pull up and the security lights came on. When I looked out the window, I noticed that it wasn't Sheila who was driving, but Jeff, Lisa's husband, who was hosting the party.

They sat in the car for a few minutes and obviously talked. Now that the security lights were on, I could see my wife clearly enough. I watched as my wife leaned the seat back as she spread her legs, pulled her dress up to her thighs and clearly displayed her white panties. She sat there for a good 30 seconds. Then she returned the seat to its normal position, got out of the car and went inside.

I met her as soon as she entered the door. She was not frightened to see me, probably because she was quite drunk. Something about what I had just seen really turned me on. I grabbed her and tried to kiss her, but she pushed me away and claimed she was too tired. I grabbed her and pushed her against the island bar in the kitchen and kept trying to kiss her. Finally I shoved my tongue in her mouth and tasted a combination of alcohol and sperm. This surprised me, of course, but not as much as what I discovered next. I reached under her dress with the intention of sliding my hand into her panties to rub her pussy; guess what her panties were missing! When I thought she was showing her panties to Jeff, she was actually showing him her naked pussy, which is completely shaved!

I was rock hard!

With no panties to contend with, my fingers easily found their way to her soaking wet pussy. I pushed two fingers inside her and fingered her quickly. In between I shoved my tongue down her throat and asked her if she fucked him. Repeatedly she said NO! I asked her further and she insisted that she had not. Then I asked her if she sucked his cock and she hesitated, a clear sign that she had done so. I asked again and still did not get an answer. I told her that I clearly tasted sperm on her breath and she finally gave in and whispered "yes". At that point my fingers were deep inside her and she was really getting into it. I pulled my fingers back, turned her around, bent her over the island bar and lifted the back of her sundress. I dipped my cock into her extremely hot pussy and began to beat her mercilessly. I didn't sleep with my wife; I fucked her like a two piece slut! When I fucked her, I growled at her for telling me what had happened to Jeff. At that point she was completely in the moment and finally agreed, but only if I didn't stop fucking her.

She said that we played and drank and drank, like always. After the games were over and the party was over, the four of us, Sheila, Lisa (the hostess, was curvy with huge breasts) and Margo (in her late twenties and no kids) went to have some more wine.

Apparently around 11:00 pm Lisa's husband Jeff came home and started chatting with us. When Sheila was ready to pack, we started to leave. Although she wasn't really ready to go, she needed a ride. Lisa offered Jeff to take her home if she wanted to stay for a glass of wine, so she gladly took her along.

I already knew from previous game nights that the conversations during their bunco nights usually included conversations about sex. She said that Jeff asked about tonight's topics as if he didn't already know, so of course we told him sex. It was all pretty harmless. Then she told me that Margo was bending down to get something out of her handbag at some point when Lisa caught Jeff staring at her bottom and asked if he enjoyed the view. His face turned red after he'd just been caught. According to my wife, she was wearing skintight white shorts. Then he said he was just trying to find out if she was wearing a G-string or had gone to the command. Margo jokingly answered that it was up to him to find out. This now became the topic of conversation, who wore what as panties. Lisa volunteered that she wore a thong, and my wife said bikini style. Margo wouldn't tell me. Finally, Jeff suggested that everyone show what they were wearing so they could find out what Margo was wearing. Margo agreed that if the others did, she'd show it.

Lisa left first because it wasn't really important to her husband. She wore a denim skirt, turned around, lifted it up and showed her thong-covered bottom. Then my wife said she did the same and showed her butt and panties. Margo put on a show by turning around and unbuttoning her shorts. She pushed them down and dropped them down to her ankles, bent over and pushed and wiggled her butt towards Jeff. Margo was wearing a G-string and took her time to pull her pants up. My wife said it was kind of exciting and funny at the same time, everyone giggled when it happened.

When I heard her recount the events of the evening, I got really excited. I pulled my cock away from her and saw how her juices completely covered my shaft. I immediately turned her around and pressed her to the floor. As she lay on her back I lifted her dress and exposed her swollen pussy. I spread her legs wide and then slammed my cock into her until it stopped. She panting loudly. When I started to push my cock in and out of her, I told her to continue her story but to look me in the eye while she told it. With a wicked grin on her face, she picked up where she left off.

The group continued to drink wine and talk about sex. Knowing Jeff, I'm sure he kept the subject of sex on purpose; I would do it. Eventually, the question of how women shave their pubic areas became a topic. Did they go naturally, did they leave a runway or did they go completely bald. Lisa volunteered that she had a runway. Margo, of course, was completely shaved, because that was the current style. My wife shocked her when she told them she was bald, too. She has a very primitive and correct image, and nobody is really aware that she was wild until the 1920s and even with me at the beginning of our marriage.

Of course Jeff wanted to see her. He really is a dog, but who could blame him. Lisa didn't hesitate; once again she lifted her skirt and pulled the top of her thong down a way to show a nicely trimmed runway without really showing her pussy. She said Margo was next, and again she made a big show by undoing her pants. She surprised us all by then leaning against the kitchen bar and lowering her shorts and thong to her knees to show a very clean pubic area. Everybody started yelling and screaming and then her attention was focused on me. My wife said that he refused and shortly after asked to leave. After several failed attempts to get her to show, Jeff finally drove her home.

The drive home took about 15 minutes. From the time they got in the car, she said Jeff kept asking her to see her shaving choices. He said they had seen the others and it was only right that she show her own shave. I'm not sure where that logic came from, but if you're not sober, it somehow made sense; so she finally agreed to show him hers. So when they came to a red light, she lifted the front of her dress, pulled her panties down to the top of her slit, turned to Jeff and spread her legs. When the light turned green, she put things back in place. Two minutes later, Jeff moved to the back parking lot of the high school and asked to see her again. She said no, but he said it was not a good look. Reluctantly, she said, as she pulled up her skirt and slid her panties down to her ankles, Jeff turned on the inside light. Then she spread her legs and turned to him. After a few seconds he couldn't control himself anymore and he reached over, rubbed her pussy and stuck his finger inside her. At this point she was so drunk and horny that she came almost instantly. Jeff unzipped his pants, pulled his cock out, grabbed her hand and put it on his cock. He started her hand in a jacking up motion and she just kept stroking him as he took his hand off hers. Then he grabbed the back of her head and pushed it down to his lap. She said she didn't fight back and began to suck him off. She said that he came in her mouth unexpectedly and she freaked out for a minute. She then opened the door and spat out his sperm.

Afterwards, she said, he closed the zipper and took her straight home. When they arrived at our house, he said he wanted to look again, so she made him do it. At the time, my wife and I were both damn wild. I couldn't hold back any longer and I pushed my dick right into her. I fell on her and pushed my tongue back into her mouth when my cock started spitting deep inside her.

I know I didn't get the full story from her that night and I've been trying to get her alone with him ever since, but she made sure that didn't happen. I'm sure something more happened. Something she's either so ashamed of or so ashamed that even a lot of alcohol combined with a good fuck couldn't get it out of her. One day I'll get the truth out of her and at least have fun doing it.

IF HE ONLY KNEW

You bubble in my mouth while your legs give way, and you share your weight between my mouth, my hand pressing your nipple, my two fingers in your pussy and the rock I leaned against when I surprised you on the way to it in the park.

"What are you doing here?"

"Fuck you!" I said with that dirty sideways smile on my face that you love and hate.

"But he's waiting for me. He has a romantic night planned. He'll want to have sex later."

As I look into your eyes and push myself into you, I say, "Well, I think you'll be well-served by our sex when he's ready.

You just gave me a dirty smile and kissed me yourself.

My hand was on your ass and my other hand was pulling your hair as I kept pushing in. I knew I couldn't hold you for too long, but I was having fun and I had you just before your third orgasm when we heard him call your name.

"Holy shit! He's looking for me!"

"I guess you'll have to be quieter then." I answered back as I pushed further inside of you.

I fucked you slower, but I used longer and harder strokes when he wondered our direction. You whispered in my ear and asked me not to say he was gone, but I kept on whispering in your ear.

"I know he's close, but I need your pussy on my dick. I need to feel your tits on my chest. I need your ass in my hand and I need to feel your breath and your teeth on my neck. Feel me inside you. Feel me putting my dick in your little pussy. Feel my warmth glow on you. Feel me fucking you. Feel me. Feel me. Feel me. Feel me fucking. "Feel me fucking you. I'll repeat how I'm ramming myself into you every word.

It does that, and you'll have an orgasm if he gets close. To stay calm, you bite my shoulder hard and ram your nails deep into my back. Then you feel my dick pounding inside you, and you know that I'm coming inside you at the same time.

We sit there as still as possible while he walks blindly past us in the dark. His feet shuffling through the leaves are louder than our hebeat breath, so he just keeps walking.

"I can't believe you did that. We could've been caught, like now, for the third time!"

"and think about it. I'll fuck you again when he goes to sleep tonight."

"Oh! You think so, huh?"

"Yeah, and when he goes to sleep, you'll come out of the tent naked and we'll do one of our marathon fucks."

"No. I can't!" They said in a desperate voice, knowing that in a few hours we'll actually fuck again.

I'll take your hand when you step out of the tent. "I hate how much I need you!" They said.

Then I say, "It's not necessity that kills me, it's how much I love you. As I lean forward and give you one of those kisses that says everything we both need to hear and feel. You melt in my arms and I lift you off the ground and walk away from your camp with you.

You fall into the mattress, the crisp sheets and soft pillows in the back of my truck and laugh that I have clearly planned this. I get up in the back and look at you with a scowl on my face.

"I told you to get naked!"

"Fuck you! I'm not running around looking for you naked. I had

I didn't know you were sitting outside my tent. We're out there all the time?"

"No! That would have been kind of creepy!" I laugh.

"Good. That would have been really kind of creepy stalker-ish." Then we both started laughing.

I have drinks and a chocolate doughnut that we can enjoy under the stars as we talk. We do this for a few minutes, and then you lean over and whisper in my ear, "Why the fuck isn't your dick deep inside me right now!

I'll throw the drink away and jump on top of you.

In a few seconds we'll be touching and sucking and groping each other like 16 year olds. You keep touching my dick and trying to get it inside you, and I won't let you. I keep teasing you so you get a hotter ending. You grab me again and lift your hips and poke your pussy on my cock and beg me to get relief.

I'll stop everything and take you in. I float above you and you feel my cock just touching your pussy. You moan "please". But I won't do it. I'm just gonna move it over your clitoris while you squirm. You can feel my warmth and my breath, but you can't reach me.

"Spread your legs as wide as you can."

Your legs shoot out until you do the splits.

"Beg."

"I need you. I want you inside me! I'll do anything if you just let me feel you inside me! Fuck me! Fuck me! Fuck me! Fuck me, fuck me, fuck me, fuck me!"

At the last "fuck me," I'm gonna drive into you with one long movement.

Can only take two or three shocks before you get your first orgasm. That night we have a happy fuck, a sad fuck, a loving fuck and a lonely fuck, but we end up with a fuck that makes the rest seem small. I sleep with you with more feelings than you know what to do and you sleep with me in the same way, but there are the unsaid things that are communicated all the time. Things like "You'll always be the one I think of when I sleep with someone else. I think about you every day. I will never stop thinking about you.

You are the love that escaped me but will never leave my heart. Always! Always! Always yours!

DOUBLE VISION

I feverishly stroked my frankfurters.

From the opposite side of the trailer - in a matching La-Z-Boy - the white trash centerfold sat naked right away, watching two soap operas, a portion of Ellen and the end of The View. All this, moments from the border to a "foreign" country.

An 18-pound cat - improperly called Tiny - took a liking to my lap and sank five razor-sharp claws into my left ball.

"Look!" concluded the race car bikini model - with tits more impressive than a supernova - joyfully. "He really likes you!"

How does burying five killing tools in one testicle equal an act of affection?

The excruciating pain made me hallucinate I was Johnathan Taylor Thomas. When I was about to faint, it was all I could do to suppress my screams.

In the end, I had eight minutes of intercourse - certainly a mercy fuck - before the woman's head began to offend her. Naked for days on end, lying in the garden in the sun - combined with a sea of margaritas - she was less interested in me than in the shitting out of a big organ.

It was then, of course, the double-wide resident who informed me about her sexual abuse as a child. Combine that with her assertions about unpredictable mood swings due to PTSD - don't ask me, damn it - and you have a recipe for the ruined rump roast I've experienced.

Had I not been involved in a multitude of erogenous heroics in the past, I would have been even more confused than Emilio Estevez at a Where's Your Career Going? seminar.

Once that was said and done, I felt lucky that I didn't end up tied up in the basement of this walking neurosis - FBI agents uncovered my rotting carcass eight months later, next to a stash of pirated copies of Shannen Doherty/Michael Caine porn tapes!

CONDOM NATION

Darla was a perfectly packaged porn prima donna who jumped into the pool with her husband - Jefe.

I slaved over the clock and ignited the conversation like a Saturn V rocket.

After many minutes of not knowing if Darla was into single men, she told all the men present that this was her second stay in a swing club. Moments later, she faked a fall on the slippery slope of the hot tub and landed comfortably on Travis' Dong - a regular guest.

At this point we ran towards her like vultures towards a carcass.

When I suggested moving Darla to the orgy bed, I was praised for my genius, as Tesla was when he invented the AC motor.

We surrounded this sexy whore in less time than it takes the IRS to ruin a life, and took turns with the said señorita while Jefe Laurie - a great time for the resident - fucked on the other end of the mattress.

I brought 14 condoms to this goddamn box spring. When I left, I managed to recover two unused prophylactics from the top of the sheet! I'm sure I didn't burn through 12 love gloves in a half-hour session, so there must be a Bermuda Triangle in this area of the club swallowing poon balloons.

I used three with Darla and two with Laurie. That leaves seven expensive latex covers lost and unexplained! In this case, I'm calling - pun intended - "Magnum P.I."

So I go back to the drugstore for supplies.

I don't mind sharing the provisions with other wasters at the pool, but most of these guys don't even show up with a single condom! It's like not bringing beer to a BYOB blowout or earplugs to a Miley Cyrus concert.

Apparently I emptied a whole bottle of lubricant during the interlude as well, as I couldn't even find the container when I left the bed!

Rubbers cost $15 per pack of 12, and cock cream costs $10. Together, that's more than the entrance fee for the swing club I frequently visit. I can't even buy the entire Matlock series on DVD for $25!

Besides, Darla's a squirter. At first I thought someone spat on me while I was sitting on her. Not knowing what it takes to make women ejaculate, it wasn't until the third time I noticed that said spring was coming out of her crotch.

Eventually Darla experienced enough circular group actions in the groin area and left the group without any possibility of contact. I always like to keep her happy, baby!

When it came to the mattress, it seemed as if the Third World War of sex had been fought on it.

I grabbed a handful of towels and a palm of hand sanitizer and cleaned exactly 12 used condoms! A coincidence? I don't think so.

TEACHING ME

This is a true story about my experience with a swinging couple. Although I wrote this story to be erotic by describing the experience as detailed as possible, this is also a way for me to actually document what happened and how I see it now, a few years later. Overall this was a very positive experience, but I will discuss some of the less than ideal details. I changed their names so as not to reveal their identity.

It was the summer after my high school graduation, and I was 18, so everything was completely legal. At that point in my almost non-existent sex life, I may have had sex once or twice, and it had been mediocre at best. But as a teenager I was horny as hell and found myself browsing the Craigslist section for casual encounters, which has since been removed from the site. I knew that my friends didn't do that, but I was quite open sexually and found it hot to be with an older couple who could show me the ropes.

Let's call them Karen and John. They were probably in their early forties, although I never actually asked them their age. They were looking for a younger man to play with them regularly. John and I were both heterosexual, so it was mainly about pleasing Karen. We exchanged a few pictures and I decided that Karen was attractive enough to meet her in real life.

Karen had a pretty face with light hair and wide hips with a pretty sexy pair of legs. Given her age and the fact that she had children, she still had a good figure. She probably had D cup breasts, but I won't pretend that she was some kind of goddess with a firm body and sassy tits. Her breasts were quite saggy and when I look back, her pussy was not nearly as tight as that of women my age. But since I was inexperienced, I didn't know that at the time and couldn't even believe that this whole thing was happening.

John was a pretty normal-looking guy and he wasn't fat or anything. It really didn't matter because he would mainly focus on Karen. I'm a pretty good looking guy with a pretty athletic body and a slightly defined jaw line along with short hair. Although I was attractive, I was quiet in class, so I didn't get much attention from the girls at school.

We decided to meet at Starbucks to talk about ourselves and discuss things before we got involved. I remember that this nervous feeling in my stomach on the ride over was a taboo.

I don't remember too many details that were discussed over coffee, but I'm sure it was all about our expectations and about ourselves. Their biggest concern was that someone would be and remain respectful so that it would become a regular thing. I think they had already had one encounter with another man before, but it had ended in the meantime. They seemed to be normal and it was easy enough to have a conversation with them. They understood that this was obviously not normal for a person my age and that I had to keep this a secret from my parents.

We decided to try and get into their minivan where we drove out of sight to an empty parking lot. While John was in the driver's seat looking out for passers-by, Karen jumped in the back seat with me.

I'm sure I was rock hard by then. Since I had been with very few other girls at that time, I was very inexperienced in pleasing a woman. But, they thought it was really hot. Karen and I started making out. She usually took the lead and used a lot of tongue to probe the inside of my mouth. After a while of kissing, she'd pull down her shirt to show off her D cup tits. As I said, they were big, but a bit saggy, with areolas half the size of a dollar. I didn't really care because I was a horny teenager and understood that this was natural for a woman her age. And hey, boobs, am I right?

She lets me fondle her breasts so that her nipples get hard. We were both really aroused.

John kept watch in the front seat while he regularly looked back to see what was going on and was obviously very aroused. He liked to make remarks about how much his wife liked it while he gave me some instructions about where to touch her and so on. It was not presumptuous, and I liked the fact that I was taught by a more experienced couple.

After making out for a while and stroking Karen's breasts, we decide to do it. She lets me slide my pants down my pants while sitting in the bucket seat of the minivan. I'm about 7 centimeters hard, a little bent and have a normal girth. I made sure I shaved completely at the bottom before I arrived. She was happy to see my rock hard member and found it super-hot that I was already leaking with foreskin.

At this point she took off her underwear and lay down on top of me. They had already told me that Karen's tubes were tied and we had agreed to do it raw, as none of us were sick. She takes my cock in her hand and slowly lowers herself, her pussy lips wrapping around the head of my cock. Gently she slides further and further down until her pussy has completely swallowed my cock. We were both in heaven and I had this "wow, this is really happening" moment.

John was also very excited to see his wife riding on a much younger man while he watched for anyone approaching the car.

She set the pace while holding on to the car seats to compensate. Since I was only 18 years old and could shoot fast, she started slowly, rocking back and forth with my tail completely inside her. She reached behind her and stroked my balls before simultaneously pulling and pushing on them, sending a stream of ecstasy through my body.

It was obvious that she was in a deep state of joy. Her breath became heavy and began to moan softly. I had not yet discovered the thrill of being more vocal and I was relatively calm, but she noticed that my mind was blown.

Her rocking back and forth increased in tempo and soon she changed to a slight up and forth movement, grabbing the handle on the window to support herself on the window and make sure she didn't bump her head against the ceiling. To my great delight, her breasts bounced up and down in front of my face. She moaned louder and more often.

John slipped into short dirty talk like "That's it, baby" or "fuck that cock". He instructed me to grab one ass cheek with each hand, which I fortunately shortened. Her riding up and down soon became even more intense as she kept sliding up my cock and banging all the way back down.

At this point I came incredibly close to the cumming and I let go a barely interpretable breath to tell her this. Seconds later waves of lust shot through my body and I felt sperm rays shooting deep into her pussy while my cock was throbbing heavily. I gasped for breath while she kept the pace until my cock was completely milked.

We all had a lot of laughs as she got off and all three of us were very happy with the result. All in all, it probably only took me a few minutes to cum as a horny young guy. But I assured them that although I came quickly, I could walk several times. While girls my age would be disappointed by the brevity, they expected this and assured me that they would take full advantage of my ability to go several rounds.

We pulled up our pants and they drove me back to my car, which was parked at Starbucks, with the full intention of meeting us for a longer session at their place.

SWINGERS CLUB

April always considered herself a good girl. She always did the right things, the kind of things that people just expect from a wife. It's not that she was happy about it, but she did it because it's what you do. The problem was that April was not thrilled about it. She really needed some excitement in her life. That started to change one night when her husband Jack took her out for a special occasion. She didn't know what it was about because there was no really special occasion to celebrate, but his excitement aroused her interest. He told her to wear something sexy. April decided to wear her black lace panties and bra under her black backless dress. It was short and revealing with a low neckline and she knew how much Jack loved how her perky tits looked in this dress.

As they drove, April had no idea where they were going. It definitely wasn't the usual restaurant they went to on weekends. Soon Jack drove to a club that looked like an older club in the middle of an industrial park. She looked at Jack reluctantly, but his confidence made her curious. ...and it wasn't long before she found out where they were. The doorman at the door looked up and down in April, and you could tell he was interested when he walked her in. It always made April a little tingly when the boys checked her out. Somehow it made her feel so sexy, so attractive, like a woman and not just like a wife. They entered the building and April couldn't believe it, her husband had taken her to a swingers club.

It was something they had talked about and something April had fantasized about, but nothing they had ever done before. A gorgeous hostess with long dark hair accompanied them into the building and gave them the introduction. Following the usual rules, they were invited to enter the dance floor, have fun and enter the private rooms that were located on the upper floor. Jack went to get drinks and April watched the scene.

The room was full of attractive people dancing in multicoloured light while the music filled the room. She didn't know where the self-confidence came from, but immediately April stepped into the middle of the dance floor. She started to dance, closed her eyes and swayed to the music hands in the air, when she suddenly felt a hand on her back. "You don't mind, do you? Would you like to dance?" April turned and saw an attractive, tall, very muscular man staring at her. His dark hair swept back, his sculpted jaw framing a beautiful smile. Without saying a word, April smiled and danced on, in front of an attractive man who was not her husband! She felt his hands moving up and down her sides as they danced. She turned and walked with her back to him, feeling his hands on her hips as she pressed her firm butt against him. It felt dangerous dancing with a stranger and April loved every minute of it. When the song ended, April turned around, gave the stranger a quick kiss, whispered "Thank you" and went to the bar.

Jack offered April a drink: "You looked sexy out there, babe, you want to explore the private rooms?" he asked. April knew she wanted to, and with a smile, the two of them went upstairs to explore what this new kind of club had to offer.

When they arrived at the top of the stairs, they found a large open area where a number of people in various forms of undress were chatting together around a large oversized bed. It looked as if it was the size of three king-size beds and was covered with red silk sheets and comfortable looking pillows. Jack and April explored a number of private rooms. Some of them were empty and consisted of a simple bedroom, while others had couples who already enjoyed each other's company. The dungeon was probably a little too much for their first time, and soon Jack and April found themselves in the large open playground.

Jack and April sipped their drinks and chatted with the other couples, singles and generally great people, which was very inviting. April felt a little adventurous and a little overdressed as everyone else seemed to be either naked or just in their underwear. April came close to Jack, her hand slipping over his cock, which was already hardened by the sexual tension in the room. "I know it's our first time here, but this place makes me so horny, Jack. Can we make ourselves a little more comfortable?" whispered April. Jack could feel April's hard nipples pressed against his chest as she whispered in his ear, and he knew immediately that tonight was going to be incredible.

Jack took April's hand and led her to the big bed. Since everyone else was either naked or almost naked, it was time to take things to the next level. Jack leaned over and kissed April passionately. His hands slowly slid down her sides, grabbed the tight black dress and pulled it over her head. April was stunning. Her perfect, crisp tits looked stunning in the soft light and the sparkle in her eyes showed Jack how excited and thrilled she was. Jack took off his shirt, slipped into his pants and joined her on the bed, naked but for his boxers. At first no one paid much attention to them as Jack and April kissed and made out on the bed, but soon a small crowd had gathered to watch and appreciate such a sexy looking couple.

"It's so hot to be watched," April whispered to Jack. "Do you think they want to see more?" she teased. Jack smiled as he knew the answer to this question. April answered by pushing Jack back onto the bed and smiling, taking off his boxer shorts, revealing Jack's already hard cock. April lowered her head and slowly licked his hard cock from root to tip. She looked up to see a crowd of about 10 people watching before she took Jack's cock in her mouth. Slowly her head bobbed and she started sucking his cock in front of a group of strangers while listening to Jack's moans. With Jack's hard cock in her mouth, April looked up to see the strangers surrounding her. Right behind her husband, a woman watched from her own chair as she played with her nipples... next to her, two men were stroking their cocks as they watched April. April stopped and looked up at them and smiled as she stroked Jack's cock. April suddenly noticed that everyone was watching this scene and she couldn't help but feel lost in the moment and get completely involved in being the center of attention...

After Jack couldn't handle it for a second longer, April took his cock out of her mouth. She slipped on the bed to kiss him and Jack could taste his foreplay on her tongue. April lay back on the bed while Jack started playing with her already wet pussy. She grabbed the red sheets in her hands while Jack's fingers slipped between her legs, making her long for his cock in her pussy. She looked up to see the group of people watching as they moved a little closer together. Some of the men already had their hard cocks in their hands and slowly stroked them.

Jack moved down onto the bed so he could taste his wife's sexy pussy. Nothing turned him on more than the taste of his wife, his tongue exploring her pussy and sucking her clitoris to make it hard. April moaned as Jack licked her pussy. April suddenly looked up and noticed the dark-haired man she had danced with before. Without thinking about it, she waved him over to her and looked down at Jack. "Jack, do you mind if my new friend plays with us?" Jack looked up and smiled. This was one of his ultimate fantasies, having sex with his wife in front of a group of people and getting another man to do it. It couldn't be better. "Absolutely," Jack said as this new man slid down next to his wife as Jack tried to lick his wife's tight little pussy again.

April couldn't help but enjoy her first time with several men. She had thought about it occasionally, but this experience surpassed everything she had imagined. April closed her eyes as this new stranger began to wrap his hot tongue around her right nipple, which made it difficult for her. Involuntarily, she pushed her pussy into her husband's face, while her nipples grew harder with every lick, tease and bite.

"I want to ride your cock," April whispered into the ear of this new stranger. He looked up and smiled. April rose quickly from her bed and kissed Jack deep. "Jack, I'm going to ride this man's tail and I want you to watch... and then cover me with your sperm!" April said with authority. Without waiting for Jack's answer, she turned and saw the beautiful stranger lying on the bed again with his legs hanging over the edge. She climbed onto the bed facing the group of onlookers while resting on this beautiful stranger. She looked behind her and saw Jack smiling and slowly stroking his thick cock before she lowered herself onto the tail of a stranger for the first time.

Without even thinking about it, April arched her back as she slowly lowered herself into the stranger's cock, the tip pressing slowly and lightly into her bald pussy - fuck she was already so wet! April moaned as she slowly rose and lowered her hips while her soaked pussy stretched to accommodate that beautiful cock. Her moans attracted a few more onlookers who surrounded her on the bed. Her hands brushed across the stranger's stomach before she slowly turned around and spun on this cock that had filled her completely. While riding this strange reverse cowgirl, she stood opposite Jack and really started riding his rooster. His moaning got louder and the stranger started to push faster. Suddenly Jack stood up and walked towards April. The stranger's thrusts were faster now, and his grunting made it clear how hard it was for him not to come. April moaned as she closed her eyes with Jack before he lowered himself to the edge of the bed and began to lick her clitoris as the stranger stabbed her in the pussy... April couldn't stand it another second and her body convulsed when she came. Her back arched back as her husband sucked on her clitoris in the specific way that seemed to prolong her orgasm while a total stranger was filling her with his sperm.

After the apparently best and longest orgasm of her life had faded away, she grabbed Jack's face and pulled it to her own "Jack I want your sperm! I want you both to cover me with your sperm!" The crowd knew exactly what was coming, and quickly took the best seats on the bed. April laid back as Jack and this stranger began furiously stroking their tails as the crowd and April encouraged them. "Come hose down for me! Hose me down on my tits! I want your sperm so bad! She moaned as both men started moaning as they both headed for their own orgasms...

It was the stranger who came first, with a moan he furiously stroked his cock while April played with his balls. Suddenly, huge spurts of hot cum burst from his cock over April's perfect tits. The stranger's moaning caused more and more strands of his hot white cum to cover April, with the cum running from her nipples and slowly down her breasts. Just as the stranger was finished, Jack moaned and his first load bounced off April's chest and hit April's cheek. Further charges shot across her chest until April's chest was covered with hot sperm.

April lay back tingling as the sperm of both men covered her chest. As both fell down beside her, exhausted and worn out, April looked at her husband and winked: "Good start, Jack. I can't wait to see how this night ends. That was definitely not our only orgasm tonight!" April looked up at the crowd around her and shouted, "Who's gonna help clean up this mess? April and

Jack both smiled when they saw several people raising their hands.

IT BEGINS

They had talked, chatted, exchanged endless e-mails and chats. Now they had agreed to meet. He was nervous, should a bull feel nervous? Being physically present was something completely different than telling her all the diabolical things he would do to her online. A culmination of weeks and months of teasing and flirting. Now it became very real.

They had agreed to meet in a different city than the one they lived in. He had arranged to spend the night in another city and she had made the necessary arrangements. A non-discreet coffee shop as the place for the meeting. He arrived there early and gave her the opportunity to look around and leave if she felt uncomfortable. He had already told her that he had no expectations, and if they did not click in flesh and blood, she had no obligation. He could not deny how nervous he was. He sat alone at the table, pretending to look at the drinks menu and checking his phone for any messages.

Then he saw them. Just like in her pictures, beautiful. Her eyes, even more stunning than in the photos. She was wearing a shimmering blue satin blouse, buttons that stuck out from her big, luscious breasts. A tight grey and black pencil skirt, just above the knee. She wore a belt around her waist and clasped her bottom and thighs. Short heels to round off the outfit, he laughed when he noticed the anklet, knowing that it said "Hotwife" on the chain. He waved, she saw him smile. His heart beat faster as she walked over, and he stood up. What should I do, hug, kiss, shake hands?

She bent over for a kiss. His hand gently touched her waist as her lips touched for the first time. A short hickey. She sat down. He sat down opposite her, yes, it just happened. Mmmm. They both smiled nervously. "How was your trip?" All the somewhat normal conversation. They ordered their coffee.

He felt the tension, this wasn't a normal conversation that was bound to happen.

"It's so good to see you at last," he said. He reached out for hers on the table, his long, slender fingers touching her shorter, delicate fingers. She looked at her hands, her nails immaculately cut and the few sunspots that were visible on her skin, at her soft, moisturizing hands with perfectly formed red nails. Then she looked at him. Her fingers closed around his. She looked into his eyes. That was all he needed to see as they both smiled, inwardly knowing that there was acceptance.

He moved his head to the side and tried to relieve the tired muscles in his neck. Spending a little time between a woman's legs can cause a man's neck to hurt. But it was worth it. He looked over at her. She was curled up on the white hotel sheets and fast asleep. He loved the shape of her body, her nice curvy ass and her full, heavy breasts. Not so long ago these breasts were on his face when she rode him cowgirl-style. They had done most of the things they had talked about in their chats.

They had started kissing her and he'd fingered her until she came. Then she gave him one of the best blowjobs of his life by allowing him to come on her face, chin and tits. She had smiled so cheekily as she cleaned herself with her fingers and licked each one clean. She told him how good her bull's sperm tasted.

She returned the favor. She spent a lot of time between her legs. She gave her the kind of tongue twisting that any good cop would do. She came twice while his tongue, lips and fingers worked on her pussy and the clitoris hurt. She pressed her thanks to his face, the wet still on the underside of the sheets.

Then they fucked. Three times that night and early in the morning. Finally, she sucked on her big breasts while riding him hard. Her legs and his cock felt the raw pain that only hard sex can cause.

Now she was asleep and he couldn't help but remove the stray hair from her face. She looked so peaceful, so content. He knew he had done his job well. Making her the center of his world, even if it was only for one night. That she experienced what it means to be a sexy and desirable woman, free from obligations and ties. To have the feeling that sex is a beautiful thing to enjoy and not an annoying duty because you expect it. He had helped her to forget her other life, even if it was only for one night. The hug, the kiss and the look in her eyes as they went to sleep were words of thanks enough for him.

STAYING WARM

It was early spring and we had decided to drive to Breckenridge, Colorado, just the four of us. Our trip to Punta Cana was a resounding success, and over time we had found a sense of comfort around us. By this time, Kathy and Tyler had been together for nearly a year, the divorce finally in its rearview and their future with us before us. We had been flirting and teasing Kathy for years at this point and Tyler and Kathy were now both comfortable enough to tease and flirt again immediately. It was simply a feeling of ease in our relationship.

So far the journey had been entertaining. We got a two-bedroom suite in one of the resort lodges in the city and took turns learning/renewing skiing, exploring the tourist town and enjoying the private Jacuzzi on the terrace of our room.

On the third day we decided to go on a trip up the mountain and try out some of the more difficult slopes. Diane had become particularly good, with very little practice, almost as if she was born for the slopes, while the rest of us tried to keep up. Diane, however, had been full of energy on this trip and would normally take me to the bedroom as soon as we left the slopes. Kathy and Tyler could often hear her moans and passionate cries as we fucked like rabbits in our bedroom.

The slopes have become quieter in recent days as the season draws to a close. As the day progressed, Diane and Tyler (who also do very well in the snow) decided that we would return to the slopes for one last time before going down for dinner. Kathy and I agreed and we headed for the ski lifts. As we reached the top of the first lift, Diane immediately led us to the next lifts, which were to take us to the Blue Diamond Difficulty Slopes in the more remote part of the mountain. We had been to this area before, so we were not worried.

As we took the last ski lift, Kathy noticed that clouds were gathering in the sky around the mountain. "Guys, we should be careful. The weather looks like it could get bad real soon."

Diane and Tyler, looking forward to their new sport, just nodded.

"I think we can make it down for our last time," I said, conveying in a somewhat firm tone the message that I was concerned but confident, "We'll get a nice hot shower when we get downstairs and then go to that new restaurant you wanted to try!

Kathy smiled and agreed, and soon we were jumping from the end of the lift and found the slopes basically deserted. The sky had darkened considerably, and we shared nervous looks.

"Let's just get going." Diane said, with a hint of doubt in her voice, "I'm sure the weather will be better once we get down. Since we had little choice at that point, we agreed and began our run.

We were perhaps already halfway down the mountain when the storm suddenly started. The visibility dropped almost to zero and we quickly stopped and found ourselves in the swirling snow. No sooner were we together than I pulled a small map out of one of the pockets of my ski equipment and studied it carefully. It looked as if there was a small emergency hut nearby.

"If we go in that direction," I shouted over the wind and pointed to the trees, "we can find shelter in an emergency hut. I reached into another bag and pulled out a short piece of nylon rope. "We should all have some of this rope in the rental equipment. Let's tie ourselves together so we won't get separated!"

The wind only seemed to get stronger as we quickly got organized, and when everything was ready, we headed for the cabin.

The door to the cabin opened and we stumbled in. Tyler slammed the heavy wooden door behind us and locked it while Kathy and Diane lit the dark room with flashlights. I don't know when the sun had set but it had darkened quickly and we barely made it to the cabin.

"Hey, I found a lantern," Tyler said from near the door and a few moments later the room was illuminated by a flickering orange glow. As we looked around we soon discovered that this shelter had obviously not been well maintained. There was enough firewood for the night, if we did not make the fire too high, but otherwise there was little else left in this place.

"Okay, folks," Diane, who took charge like a tough woman, began, "here's the plan. Let's get out of these wet clothes before we get sick and get the fire going. While you guys build the fire, Kathy and I will see if we can take stock of what we have here. Kathy nodded, and we all agreed.

In a few minutes Tyler and I had lit the fire nicely and the girls went back to spread blankets. We were all still in our ski outfits from before.

"We have some small blankets," Kathy began, "but we'll probably just have to huddle together. She pointed to the small pile of firewood. "Will this last the night?"

"If we're willing to make ourselves comfortable and share body heat, sure." I said for sure. "If it doesn't, it won't. I could go back and cut more if I had an axe, but I don't see that we have a choice."

Diane took the lead once again. "Mike, help me out of bed," she said, and I took Diane's side. It wasn't long before she came out of her ski outfit, only to discover she was wearing very sexy black underwear underneath. "I wanted to surprise you later," she said, "I didn't know we were going to be in a survival situation!

"Damn, woman!" Kathy said loudly from where she was sitting by the fire, "I've never seen you in that dress before, is that new?

The outfit was a dark red bra and panty set, the bra very transparent... almost completely transparent... and the panties were a string bikini set tied at the sides. When I started to reach for her, Diane suddenly knocked my hands away.

"Don't touch me with your cold, cold appendages." She laughed. "Take off your outfit and warm me, husband!"

I saw a glimmer of mischief in her eyes and I liked what I saw. I undressed quickly and went to my boxer shorts. Catcalls rang out from the other side of the room and I looked up and saw Kathy and Tyler in a dress similar to ours. Kathy was wearing a dark blue bra and panties, both pointed and tasteful at the same time. Tyler had switched to the same brand of boxer shorts as me almost 6 months ago so we fitted together a bit.

Diane and Kathy grabbed the blankets and we all made some adjustments by lying on the floor side by side. We adjusted to the women in the middle and lay down on the outside of the floor. In the kitchen drawer, two sets of spoons were facing each other.

As Diane turned against me and tried to make herself comfortable she said, slowly lifting her gorgeous bottom against me, breathing softly and making little excited noises. I could see that Kathy seemed to be doing the same with Tyler and both women stared deeply into each other's eyes.

"'You two are so hot', Kathy said throatily whispering.

"So are you,' Diane returned in a seductive voice. She reached out and ran along Kathy's side with one hand, playing gently with her skin.

Kathy shifted slightly forward and her lips met Diane's. As they kissed, Tyler and I continued to rub slowly against our partners and occasionally caressed the kissing women. Kathy's hands went to Diane's breast and I felt and pinched her nipples through her top so I did the sensible thing and unfastened Diane's bra for her. It was gone in seconds, both women pulled it away and suddenly Kathy's lips were on Diane's breast.

I watched as Tyler pulled quickly, unhooking Kathy's bra and spraying her tits for all to see. Diane did not miss the opportunity to return the favour and soon licked and sucked and then ran her teeth across Kathy's nipples. Both women crunched their hips on their husbands and we both began to stab each other against our wives.

Diane felt my cock harden against her, turned away from Kathy and climbed on top of me, kissed me deeply and slipped against my hardness. With a smile Diane glided down and pulled my boxer trunks with her and freed me from her shackles. When my cock came in sight she grabbed it and began to slide her hands up and down its length, a throaty groan that rose deep from her inside as she looked at the object of her desire.

A moan on the side made both Diane and I look as Kathy's head bobbed over Tyler's tail. She sucked him deep like an expert and his hands were buried in her thick hair, her face pulled down on him. Diane let out her own soft moans and followed him, matching Kathy blow for blow to my massive cock.

After a few moments of this they kissed each other, never stopped stroking each other and started whispering to each other. Tyler and I could not hear what was being said but they seemed to agree. Before either of us could react, they suddenly changed sides. Kathy's hand wrapped around my hard cock as Diane grabbed Tyler and started sucking it.

As I felt Kathy's lips slide over my cock I almost exploded. I looked down and watched in amazement as she sucked it with passion and skill as my wife did the same to the man next to me. This went on for several more minutes before Kathy and Diane took over again.

Diane ordered Tyler to slide closer to me until we were close together and then, without saying another word, she reached for his cock, spread it open and sat on it. Without thinking, he began to push himself into her and her moans filled the room.

My attention was suddenly distracted when I felt Kathy move above me. The next thing I remember is her lowering herself onto my cock and sitting on it right next to Diane. They both started rubbing against our tails and we both did our best to keep up. As they rode on us, Kathy and Diane kissed and played with each other's tits, constantly trying to please each other.

Kathy and Diane both came several times, their orgasms rocking through Tyler and me and sending us to incredible new heights of pleasure.

After a few minutes Tyler announced he was approaching and both women climbed down from us. Kathy lay down on the floor facing Tyler and Diane climbed onto her, her breasts pressed together. Tyler turned to his side and both grabbed his cock, sucking and stroking it between them in turn. When I saw them lying there, both bare before me, I decided I was not finished. I slipped over and shoved my cock into Diane's dripping pussy while she was lying on top of Kathy.

We held out for a long time as Kathy and Diane alternated between sucking and stroking Tyler while I fucked them both and reached into one and then the other for a few strokes.

Suddenly, Tyler moaned and came, covering Diane and Kathy with thick ropes from the sticky mess. I was not far behind and soon I was standing over them and came up on their tits as they squeezed them.

Kathy bent over and licked the sperm off Diane's tits and she returned the favour. Suddenly exhausted from a day of skiing and a night of passion, we all fell asleep in a big heap on the floor next to the fire.

OUR FIRST TIME

V and I have been together for almost 31 years now. We met in the second years of our undergraduate program. A few years after starting our professional career, we were married and then settled down in our life on the outskirts of town - three children and a dog.

It was in April 2003, after dinner, when V and I watched the episodes "Everybody Loves Raymond" and "Who's Next". In this episode, Ray Romano and his wife choose partners for each other in the event of their death. (Truly, it's one of the funniest episodes ever aired, and one that has changed our lifestyle in the months and years to come).

A few days later we were on a road trip to Ann Arbor, MI. During the trip we discussed the episode again and laughed again. The conversation turned to us, and we started to joke that we would apply it in our lives. I clearly remember her asking me who I would choose for her. A few miles later I told her that I had chosen my brother - R - for her. She in turn chose her widowed sister - J - for me.

I was not surprised that she chose me, for she knew that I liked J very much; however, she had a naughty smile on her face when she heard that R could be her mate when I came by. After that day, we talked little about our discussion, but I was fascinated by the look on her face when she heard my choice for her.

My brother and I are very close. When we were younger, we used to share girls. He often told me that V was the one who got away and that he was very jealous of me. I also had a weakness for his wife - K - but I always kept my thoughts to myself to avoid complications.

In the course of 2003, after many conversations with my brother "R", I informed him of my decision for my wife. He confessed that he would also like to love her and suggested that we should exchange spouses. I knew that he would easily convince his wife - K. I had the challenge to bring V into the game.

The day before Thanksgiving 2003, we planned a surprise visit to my brother and his family. V was alarmed by the unexpected visit and was desperate to organize the event.

R, K, and I planned and knew the purpose of the visit; V did not know. The children were happy to meet their favorite uncle, aunt, and cousins. That night I broke it to V that I shared Ray Romano's "Who's Next" conversation with R and K; that R was very much in love with them. V was stunned, but I could see the same smile returning to her face.

Thanksgiving Day, as planned, K and I stayed in our rooms intentionally longer. R went down early and started working on V. When I went downstairs, R was in the kitchen with V, helping with the dishes. He gave me a hidden thumbs-up, the same sign we gave each other when we were younger. The day went by quickly and soon we were by the fireplace, children in their rooms and the dog at the door.

V lay in my arms; K and R snuggled up together. R moved towards us and took V by the hand. She followed his lead. K and I saw them close their bedroom door behind them.

K smiled and unbuttoned her blouse. I sat down next to her and for the first time, my hands reached into her blouse and unbuttoned her laced bra, my mouth hitting hers. Her tongue rolled on mine as I unhooked her bra to release her D-cup shaped breasts. Her dark nipples were erect, her legs apart as she leaned back on the couch. I could smell her wet panties.

I got up and bent over and took her petite body in my arms. I kissed her and carried her into our bedroom. As we passed her room, K wanted us to hear through her door. I gave in and we put our ears to the door. There was a soft, soft moaning and groaning. We could feel the passion in the air.

We entered our room and I put K on the bed that V and I shared all our lives. I stood against the door when I saw K drop her clothes and lay down on the bed, folding her legs up to her knees and parting her hairy pussy. She said softly, "I had a brother, let me see what you have to offer.

I got down on my knees and held her ass tight, I stuck my nose in her cunt. I smelled her and her wet dripping cunt approached me. My tongue was whipping inside her and it got loud. She moaned as she pushed my hair into her cunt. She lifted her hips and lifted her ass from the bed while I held my mouth firmly on her vagina. She squirted with a scream and went on loud as she almost fell off the bed.

I heard a knock at the door. I left K on the bed. I wiped my wet face and went to the door. My brother looked in and said, "Boys, keep it down. V is worried that the kids might hear us." R peered in to see his wife gasping for breath. I looked at him with a silent examination. He looked at me, "She's asking me to use protection.

I laughed. I asked him to wait in the room. I went over to the room where V was. She was sitting by the bed, in an open bathrobe. I sat next to her and whispered to her, "If you don't want to, I'll understand." She looked at me and said, "No, that's not it."

Just then, R and K came in. K was naked. R closed the door and began to undress. K got down on his knees and took R's cock in his mouth. V watched

her. R gestured V to come closer. She obeyed and knelt down as well. R moved away from his wife's mouth, and stood a full 7 inches straight in front of V. V turned around to see me now standing naked by the bed.

Crawled to me and had my manhood in her mouth. My brother held V's head and began to fuck her mouth gently. I leaned back on the bed and K moved with me and wouldn't let go. The room was filled with sounds of oral sex. I closed my eyes as K went to work.

I felt the bed move. I opened my eyes to see V lying next to me, her legs on R's shoulders and her left hand clasping my right hand. She looked into my eyes as R was gently pushed into them. It was thick, hard and deep inside her. Unlike K, she moaned softly with an aaah! that escaped her gnashing teeth. K mounted me and rode me while she pushed her dark nipples through her fingers.

Passion filled the air. I could see the joy on R's face. V held his own. K was Cumming again. I had to pull her to me to muffle her screams with my mouth. I held her while my hard cock dug deep into her tight, wet pussy. My thighs were wet and the sheets were soaked from her splash.

My brother moved to V, and the whole body began to fuck my wife slowly and passionately. Her hand released her grip on mine and circled on his back, her legs around his ass as he moved in and out of her.

The bed rocked. I stood on the edge, R. V. trembled, her thighs tightened around R. R was the first to shoot his sperm into my wife. The exhausted K rolled over to my side, her hands, which grabbed my cock, began to twitch me violently. V moaned and her nails dug into the back of R. R emptied his balls into V. The trembling body of V was held down by his heavy frame. He whispered into her ear: "I love you, V, I love you like my own child".

V replied with a warm embrace: "I love you too, R, I love you as my own child.

K and I looked at her while K continued to milk my thick erection. V, R and K looked back at me as my cock exploded into the air and fell onto my belly and the firm grip of K. V saw K take the sperm in her hands and lick it clean.

V looked at me for the first time in many days and smiled. I could see that she loved me more now than that morning.

THE BOUNCER

Having sex in the toilet of a bar has always been on my "fuck list", but it never seemed like I would get the chance. They tend to design bathroom doors so that they can tell when two people go into one or when someone goes into the wrong one. Either the bar is far too crowded, there is never an opportunity to sneak into the men's room with my boyfriend, or it is too slow for the bartenders to notice.

Not to mention all those fears of getting caught. One night, however, we felt brave enough to do it. Why not? We decided to go to a bar we had never been to before and which we would never go to again if we were caught. We sat together, had a drink and knew what we would do, it was like a third presence between us.

We couldn't stop touching each other, but we didn't want to make it too obvious that we were so aroused. After a few drinks we felt tipsy enough to go for it, we didn't care if we got caught. It definitely seemed as if we snuck into the men's room without anyone noticing and there was no one else in there.

We went to the stall and immediately started making out, our hands exploring each other's bodies to the fullest. I took off my thong and put it in his pocket and rubbed his hard cock over his pants. We moaned and forgot for a moment that we had to be quiet in case someone came in. I put my finger on my lips to shut us both up and pulled his cock out of his pants. I stroked him and his fingers went under my skirt and rubbed vigorously against my clitoris. I moaned softly into his mouth and then urged him to sit on the toilet.

I pulled up my skirt and turned around to shake my bottom and tease him. He grabbed him hard and started to finger me from behind. I began to tremble, the pleasure was almost too much to keep calm and I was almost too tipsy to care.

I leaned back and maneuvered my ass to sit slowly on his hard cock, with my pussy practically dripping on him. We both couldn't help but moan softly as I sat down completely and felt him fill me completely. I started jumping and rubbing myself against him quickly. He wrapped an arm around me and started rubbing my clitoris. I spread my legs on both sides of him and allowed myself to concentrate on nothing but pleasure. We remained surprisingly calm.

A man came in and I quickly stopped hopping on his tail and wanted to keep still until the man had left. But my friend had another idea. He grabbed my hips and forced me to rub against him, just lifting me up and down a little. It felt so good that I covered my mouth with my hand to hold back the moaning.

The man left shortly after he came in and I started jumping again strongly as soon as he was gone. I couldn't take my hand off my mouth, it felt so damn good to be completely still. We were in the middle of the pleasure when another man came in. I slowed down, but I didn't stop bouncing up and down.

Next thing we saw, however, was that we stopped about two metres in front of our stable door. And he knocked. "Bar Security." A rogue said from the other side of the door. We froze immediately. "Listen, we know what you're doing in there, and I have to throw you out. Get dressed and come out." He didn't go away from the stable door, just stood there and waited for us.

I tried to tear myself away from my friend, but he grabbed me by the hips and slammed me back on his dick. "Let's invite him in instead." He whispered in my ear and he moved me up and down by himself. I kept jumping up and down and bending over to unlock the stable door. I swung it up slowly and stared the bouncer right in the eyes as I continued to move up and down.

"We'll go right after, we promise," I began. "But how about coming to us first?" I winked and let the pleasure appear on my face as I rode on my friend. He stared at us in shock, not knowing what to do. "What can it hurt?" My friend shouted to him. The doorman paused only half a heartbeat before he squeezed himself into the cabin with us and closed the door behind him.

Damn, he was getting hard already. I felt him stiffen under my hand as I rubbed it through his pants. I pulled up my shirt to show him my tits and he touched them while he saw me riding a cock in front of him. I took his hardening cock out of his pants and gently stroked it. For a moment I thought about condoms, but the excitement of all this threw this thought to the winds. My friend continued to rub my clitoris while he pressed me hard on his cock.

I felt the orgasm bubbling inside me and I quickly stroked the now hard cock of the bouncer as it exploded above me. My friend reached his climax at the same time and reached out to cover my mouth with his hand when we both came. I moaned loudly into his hand, unable to stay calm and unable to concentrate on anything around me. When my orgasm subsided and I came to, I was still stroking the doorman. My boyfriend lifted me up and off him and the bouncer grabbed me to turn around me. He pushed me on his back to turn around and I grabbed my friend's shoulders to keep my balance.

The bouncer lost no time before he stuck his whole cock into my soaking wet cunt. His hands grabbed my hips tightly and he drove into me and sent me rocking back and forth, close to my friend's face. My mouth hung open and screamed softly at the intensity. My boyfriend gave me a wicked smile and loved how much I enjoyed being fucked by a complete stranger.

When my second orgasm began, I bent over to kiss my friend deeply, partly in lust over the complete falsity of the whole thing, partly to muffle my screams again. The bouncing of the doorman became more irregular and went crazy on this unique occasion. He moaned softly as he retreated and came with my whole back, my shirt pulled up, and I even felt some of his semen hitting the back of my head. He sighed and let his cock rest on my ass. "Goddamn, you're perverted."

We laughed and kissed again. "I guess we are." I said, smiling and looking at him. "We're getting off now." We left the bar, hand in hand, with dried cum in our hair, and the two bartenders gave us reproachful looks. It was fantastic.

THE RIVER

I am sure that nobody will believe this, but it is a true story, it happened many years ago, and everyone involved was much more than of age, in fact nobody was under 40 years old.

The only real reason I am writing this down at all is because my wife and I spent many years as swingers and had many great adventures, and now that I am old and in very poor health and she has died, I thought I might try to write down at least some of our more unusual events and tell others about them and show them how much fun we had. I have never tried to write anything down before. So if you can't stand bad spelling and even worse grammar, please stop reading this and go fuck yourself. I'm not writing these stories in any order, only the ones that come to mind.

Many years ago my wife and I were visiting her mother, she comes from a large family and most of her brothers and sisters were there as well. I was out on the back deck talking to one of her brothers when I heard her eldest brother mention that he had found a really good place by the river where you could have a lot of fun.

He talked about a nice swimming spot, great fishing, camping and a very active toilet with glory holes.

I tried to pay close attention, but to make it look like I was involved in another conversation. As I listened, I realized that this would be a great place for my wife, we had been swingers for many years and she loved glory holes.

I had to think about the situation for a while to decide how best to proceed.

I saw the chance to make a perverted fantasy come true.

I told my wife about the place after we got home and that I thought we should see it and she agreed, and since it was only a few miles from our home, we got ready and set off. It took us about 45 minutes to get there, and her brother was right, it was a nice little place, far off the beaten track, with lots of parking, a nice river and a toilet on the edge of the forest.

We parked the car, looked around a bit and then walked up to the toilet. It was small, one door on one side for men and one on the other side for women, we went to our respective sides to have a closer look, there were 2 stands, a urinal and a sink on my side, each stand had a Glory Hole leading over to the women's side and a Glory Hole leading into the other stand next to it.

I could see light through small holes in the outside walls, probably peepholes, and much to my surprise there was a skylight. I was just getting ready to leave the toilet and see what my wife Julie had found on her side of the toilet when the door opened and a black man came in, smiling and going into the back stall.

I hadn't heard that my wife had left her side of the toilet and I was really hoping she was still inside. In order not to mess up a possible funny encounter, I stepped out and went around the outside of the building.

I tried to be as quiet as possible when walking, and although they were hard to see, I found peepholes drilled into the wall on the woman's side. I quickly found the peephole when I looked into the rear cabin of the woman's room.

I could see my completely naked woman on her knees sucking her black cock.

She sucked his big fat cock for about 10 minutes, then she put her ass in the hold for a good fuck, they fucked hard for several minutes, then he shot his load of hot cum into her tightly shaved pussy.

She gathered her stuff together and we drove home, we talked about everything and decided to come back as soon as possible.

I had heard her brother say that he likes to go there on Friday nights just before dark, so I mentioned to Julie of course that I thought Friday would be a good time to go, and of course I didn't mention her brother at all or what he said. When Friday finally came, we went there again, we got down early enough for her to swim and have time for a short picnic. She wore a sun dress, a very short sun dress and nothing else.

She went to the small toilet three times while we, well, I guess I waited, because she didn't know about my perverted little plan, she waited until a guy went to the toilet, and then she went in on her side, and yes, she sucked all three cocks and fucked one of them.

Finally just before dark I saw her brother's truck pull in, he parked near the toilet and went in, I smiled and looked at Julie.

"Looks like another customer, honey."

She smiled and walked towards us, we were on the women's side of the toilet, a good place not to be seen and a good place to listen for cars up close. I waited a few minutes and then went as quietly as possible to a peephole. There she was, completely naked in the back booth, one arm running through the Glory Hole and feeling her good, squeezing her tits and ass and then sticking a finger in her pussy. I couldn't believe my luck, I had to sneak over and make sure it was actually her older brother Don at the Glory Hole, and it was.

I slipped back to the peephole on her side, she had a tit through the hole and loved to get sucked on her nipple and bitten, then he put his cock through the hole, he was huge, at least ten centimetres and very thoughtful. She jerked him for a few seconds, then she opened her mouth and pushed him in, he moaned as his dick head came into his little sister's mouth.

Julies is an experienced cocksucker and has had a lot of practice in getting big cocks into her tight little neck. She pushed and turned her throat around her big brother's cock while he encouraged her with his words all the time.

"That's it, bitch. Suck my dick, take it all down, you little whore."

It took a while, but his dick went up to the balls in her throat. She came by just sucking his dick, and soon it was down her bitch's throat.

I thought the show was over and I was pretty glad that my evil plan had worked out so well, but no one came out of the toilet, I went back to the peephole and found her ass plastered up to the hole and the sound of him banging against the wall as he fucked her hard and naked.

I was so excited, I almost splashed into my jeans, but I stayed calm so as not to spoil the conversation.

They must have fucked for half an hour, she moaned and came repeatedly every few minutes, finally he let out a deep groan and filled his little sister's pussy with hot thick brother juice.

I went back to my hiding place at the edge of the forest, soon after Julie came over and walked a little funny.

"How did it go?" I asked.

"Wonderful," she said.

We rested on a bench down the path for a few minutes and she told me the whole story without realizing that I had been watching the whole thing.

Her brother had left while we rested and talked, then we went back to the car and drove home.

"Do you think you would like to do that again?" I asked.

She smiled with a stupid, freshly fucked smile and said.

"He wants to do it again next week, he's going to fuck me in the ass next time."

I was shocked.

"Do you want his dick in your asshole?"

"Yes," she said.

At first I didn't know how to go on from here, I mean, I was gonna tell her what happened, but now I had the chance to let her brother fuck her in all three holes. Guess which one I chose.

JULIA'S TREAT

A street lamp flickered when I drove the cherry-red 67 Ford Mustang convertible through the never-ending suburban streets. It was late, all houses were dark and the curtains were drawn. Nothing moved, except maybe a raccoon in the backyard trying to steal food from someone's garbage.

Julia and I had flown to New York by air. We were trying to save some money on our big American vacation while we still wanted to treat ourselves. So I rented the classic Mustang, a car I'd always wanted to drive.

"How lost do you think we are," Julia said as she looked out the car window at the endless procession of driveways and houses.

"Pretty lost, these streets all look the same to me." The downside of a vintage car is that there's no sat nav to help you find your way, you're back to old-fashioned maps and written directions. We didn't have those either.

When we approached a "Stop" sign at a crossing, I could see that there were no cars coming from any direction. It seemed pointless to stop just to drive away again immediately, so I just kept on rolling. The sudden flashing of the blue lights of a police car told me that I had made a mistake.

The police interceptor appeared behind me and I stopped at the edge of a quiet road that looked just like every other road we had driven on in the last hour. In the rearview mirror, I watched as the New York State Police got out of his car and slowly approached my window.

"Maybe we can at least ask him for directions," Julia said.

He knocked on the window, and I rolled it down.

"Is this your car, sir?" he asked.

"It's a rental, my girlfriend and I are on vacation, but we're a little lost, could you..." He cut me off.

"License and registration," he said.

I reached over Julia and reached for the glove compartment. The policeman shone his flashlight into the car, at first I thought he wanted to help me, but it seemed as if the beam rested on Julia's legs more than the open compartment. She was wearing a short pleated skirt, which she showed off, and together with long socks it was a look that I found extremely cute.

"I can't find the registration, Officer," I said.

"Would you please get out of the car?"

"It's a rental, maybe they have it, I could call them?"

"Both of you, step out of the car."

We did as we were told, Julia came and stood beside me in the street. The policeman had one hand resting on his gun.

"Okay, turn around and put your hands on the roof of the car." ·

We'd both seen a lot of cop movies, so we knew what he meant. We turned around and put our hands flat on the roof, feet apart. He came towards me first and kicked against my shoes, so my legs were spread wider. He checked me for a hidden weapon, patted my chest and waist belt, but kept an eye on Julia, who stood next to me stiff as a poker. He turned to her and stood close behind her, almost between her legs, his mouth close to her neck.

"Spread them," he said.

She tried, and he shook her hand and pushed her knees further apart with his own. Then his hands were on her. He started at her waist and led her up the sides, then all the way around to the front where they touched her breasts. I felt something stirring inside me, not jealousy or anger, but excitement. He took a step back and crouched down to grope for something in her sock. Slowly his hands slid up her leg until they had left the sock behind, stroking the bare skin of her thighs and continuing upwards until they touched the hem of the skirt. They went on until they reached the very top. Julia let out a little squeak, I suspected he must have lost his leg.

"Well, what have we here?" he said. Then he opened the door on the driver's side and turned to me.

"Get in the car and put your hands on the steering wheel where I can see them. If you so much as twitch, you'll both spend the night in the cells."

I did what I was told. He took the key out of the ignition and locked the door.

"Now you," he said to Julia, "put your hands behind your back." She was handcuffed, and I began to wonder what that policeman was up to. It didn't take me long to wonder. He took the club from his belt and turned Julia around with it until she was facing him. Then he hooked it over her shoulder and pushed her down until she was forced to kneel under the pressure. Her head was at the same level as my window when she knelt face back on the street. I saw her licking her lips involuntarily, and if the policeman had any doubts, that was probably the end of it. I heard him unzip his fly and had a great view as he thrust the head of his thick cock into Julia's mouth. As she greedily sucked his cock, I felt my own stiffening. Watching this stranger using my friend's mouth gave me a great thrill.

The policeman put his hand on her head and pulled her towards him, his cock filling her mouth. He put the nightstick behind her neck, holding her head close to his crotch. Julia's head swayed back and forth, sucking and slurping. I could hear the policeman moaning with pleasure, she was an excellent cocksucker, the best I had ever known, so I didn't have to guess how good it would feel for this renegade policeman to have her warm, wet mouth serving him. I was so aroused that a tingling sensation ran down my back.

It seemed as if he was going to come off pretty quick, I know I would have done it too. But his self-control was better than mine. He let go of Julia's head and stepped back. His cock slipped out of her mouth with a wet "pop".

I watched as he hooked his arms under hers and lifted her onto her feet. He turned her around and bent her over the hood of the car. His hands lifted her skirt over her bottom to reveal her tight red panties. He tore them off and threw them to the side.

With one hand he pressed her back, his other hand led his cock into her pussy and gave a satisfied grunt as the thick head opened her. He pushed it all the way into her until it was pressed against her. Then he began to fuck. No preamble, no build-up, just raw fucking. He pulled his cock out and slammed it back in, harder and faster each time, until he hit her pussy so hard that the car bounced up and down on the suspension.

The sensitive head of my cock rubbed against my shorts and I felt like I might cum if he would just fuck her long enough. With the window open I could hear how wet she was, I could hear him grunting at every deep push, and I could hear her moaning with relish as he refuelled her.

The knocking grew stronger as he put both hands on her ass cheeks, he pumped his cock mercilessly into her. Then the pace slowed down, I could see that he was about to come by pressing deep into her pussy and reluctantly sliding out again. I could feel the orgasm building up in my own balls as he pushed himself into her once more and emitted a long, satisfied moan. He collapsed on top of her and pressed her to the hood as he softened inside her.

After what felt like an age, he regained his strength and dismounted from her. He took off her handcuffs and threw the car keys through my open window. Then he lifted Julia's panties off the floor.

"I'll keep them for now, but maybe next time I'll let you earn them back," he said.

The policeman drove away when Julia got back in next to me.

"Shit, are you okay?" she said.

"That was intense. I've never been so excited in my life," I said.

"You're not upset?"

"Of course I'm not angry, well, it's just that you stopped before I could come too."

"Maybe I can help you with that," she said, "but let's get out of here first."

I turned the key in the ignition and drove off. The image of my beautiful girlfriend bent over the car, the thought that he came in her and how skillfully she had sucked his cock shot through my mind again and again. My rock hard cock continued to tent my shorts. Julia must have noticed it when she put her hand on me and squeezed me before she opened my zipper and freed me.

15 stories: BROKEN IN!

15 Forbidden Sex Stories of Submissive Sex, Raunchy BDSM and Tantric Sex

Rose Reed

Table of Contents

THE TOWN SWINGERS

I had just moved to this town. With my pension money, I bought a house in the neighborhood. I tried to get used to my new surroundings and a new life. The life I had known all these years was a hectic one. I drove to work at 6:00 a.m. and arrived home at 7:00 p.m. My three children have grown up, and all of them had a successful career each. My wife would spend her time with them. A few months, each of them leaving me practically alone.

My wife called to tell me that she would be with me for Christmas. That would be in six months. In the meantime, I tried to find a good restaurant in town. I was afraid of those fast food places. It took me a week to find a decent restaurant. This restaurant happened to be the cheapest. That's why I often came here for my meals. Soon I became familiar with it.

Every day a group of four decently dressed gentlemen had lunch here. They all looked well over 60 years old. They discreetly discussed some business, it seemed to me. They could be certain CEOs or boards of directors. In any case, I was not at all interested in their business. As a pensioner, I was paid not to work. So I saw myself from such an interesting angle.

One afternoon, I came here for lunch. These four gentlemen were here earlier. They had finished their lunch. By the way they sat, I knew they had had their talks. I noticed that during their discreet discussion they were all sitting with elbows on the table. They would lean back as soon as their discussion was over.

I came in and looked for an empty table. As I walked past them, they nodded at me. I returned their gestures with a smile. Their eyes followed me. I gave my order and waited. After I was served by a waitress, I started to eat. A waiter came to my table and informed me in a low voice that my bill had been paid by these gentlemen. I looked up and nodded at them. They smiled back.

The next day I came back for lunch. I was just about to sit down when a waiter came up to me to tell me that these gentlemen had invited to their table. I did not want to offend them and went to their table. The same waiter took our order. We shook hands and introduced ourselves. They were pensioners like me, too, not CEOs or boards of directors, as I suspected earlier. The food came. We ate and talked like old buddies. We had so much in common. In a flash, it seemed like we'd all known each other for ages. The date was set. The next day we would have lunch together again.

That evening my wife called to see how I was doing. I cheerfully told her about my new-found friends. She was happy for me and would like to meet them one day. She told me that our grandchildren are as naughty as ever. She had so much fun babysitting. I told her I was looking forward to having lunch with these gentlemen again.

After two weeks of having lunch with these gentlemen, they invited me to have lunch with them every Friday night. They would all get together with their wife once a week. I told them that my wife was not with me at the moment but would be here for Christmas. They insisted that I join them tonight and bring my wife later. It was just dinner for a change. I agreed.

At 7:00, I drove into town and waited for them. Soon they arrived in four cars. There were nine of us. These gentlemen came with their wives. Their wives were all gray-haired, plump grandmothers. These grandmothers were high-spirited. They were very friendly and cheerful. We got our cars together and drove to our host, whom I had never met before.

We arrived at a house 7 km from the city. An old man stood at the door to welcome us. He was tall and bearded. I was introduced to him by the others.

We shook hands and he took me to his house. There were only three people in the house, our bearded host, his wife and an old mummy. His wife was a great lady in the 70s. Her maid was a chubby maid in the '60s. Because of her kindness and the hospitality of our host I quickly found myself in this circle of friends.

Dinner was served, and the menu was contributions from everyone but me. Tonight I was her guest. I would probably have to make a contribution next Friday. During dinner, the conversations focused on me. I was new here, so there was so much to talk about. They were really polite people, and they were interested in everything I told them. They even wanted me to describe my wife. After what I told them, they all agreed that my wife should be a very good and interesting person. So they were all looking forward to meeting her.

After dinner we all go into the spacious living room. Wine was served. The gentlemen sat opposite the ladies. The ladies seemed to be a happy bunch. They giggled, giggled and laughed. The men seemed very obliging. They agreed on everything. Then our host went over to his hi-fi system to play soft music.

Then everybody got up except me and started to waltz. The plump maid came over and invited me to waltz with her. And when I got up to waltz with her, everybody clapped. We danced the waltz to the next melody. Then we all changed partners. The host's wife took the maid's place. We were on the same level. As we danced on, she held me closer with each moment. Her sagging breasts were flat against my chest. I looked around and saw everyone dancing intimately. The host danced with one of these elegant grand- mothers. They kissed very intimately. Before I could react, her lips took mine. Her tongue felt my lips, and I let her go in and curl my tongue.

Soon our bodies were pressed flat against each other. I felt her pussy pressed hard against my dick. She fucked me a little. I felt guilty for dancing like that when her hus- band was in the same room. But everyone else was doing the same. The music stopped and everyone went out for a drink of wine. I followed exactly what they were doing. The next melody started. Once again we swapped partners. This time I danced a waltz with a granny with rosy cheeks. She was much smaller. Her head hardly reached my chin. With one arm around her shoulder we moved only in steps and in rhythm. She had one arm around my waist. She squeezed me a little tight and her other hand moved first around my belly and then down to my cock. She rubbed my cock as it slowly came to life. I was in a state of confusion as to whether I should do or refuse these advances.

All these moments of caressing made me concentrate on my dance partner. I raised my eyes to see what was happening to the others. I was more than shocked to see our host sitting on the sofa while an unidentified grandma gave him a headbutt. Another couple did something standing up. I couldn't see what they were doing because their backs were to me. One gentleman leaned against the wall while our host's wife gave him a hand job. They all had their clothes on, and just like me, only our tails were sticking out.

My partner with the pink cheeks jerked me off with her pink fleshy hands. Every now and then she touched my concoction.

While I was standing there staring and getting my dick jerked, someone leaned against me. I turned my head and saw a gentleman doing something to his partner that I could not see. Another couple got bolder, they stripped naked and the grandmother had to sit on the sofa while her partner gave her oral sex. Soon they were all naked, leaving me and my partner fully dressed.

My partner unbuckled my belt and helped me to take off my pants. I also helped her to take off her pants. I watched as her big sagging breasts fell down as I undid her bra. Since she was fair-skinned, her tits were pink and slightly wrinkled. I looked down but could only see her belly. Her pussy was hidden under her big belly. She knelt down and started sucking my cock. She went down so far and licked my balls. Soon I felt her tongue go further down. I spread her legs to leave enough room for her head so her tongue could reach my asshole. Her tongue probed my asshole and gave me the pleasure I had never experienced before.

I knelt down with her on the floor. I let her rest on all four limbs and the dog fucked her. Her hands reached for my balls from below. Soon another couple joined us. The man knelt in front of the grandmother with the rosy cheeks, which I pumped up from behind. He forced her to suck his cock. His partner then stood over the granny I was fucking. She pushed her pussy in my face and asked me for an oral. I tried to stick my tongue in her slit but couldn't get deep enough. She had thick semen in her pussy and I still had to lick her.

I gave up on that granny. Fucking her was no fun at all. Her stretched out old pussy was soft and loose. I stood up to the granny I was licking. We kissed while I stroked her soft tits. Her tits hung flat on her chest. It looked like skin that had been folded and hung loose. I took my cock to her pussy. She lifted one thigh, which made it easier. The penetration was easy. She had one hand holding up her leg like a heron in the shallow water while the other hand was wrapped around my waist. A granny came and licked my balls and her pussy. It was interesting. This granny had a lot of sperm. Fucking standing up was tiring for old goats like us. When I kept fucking her, she started moaning. I couldn't be sure if she was faking it. If she put her arm around my waist, it could probably be a signal for her Cumming. I took out my cock and I put my fingers inside her pussy. Yeah, she came. I could feel her pussy pulsing.

As I was tired, I went to the sofa. Our host's wife came to me. She sat down next to me and began to kiss me. With her hands she worked on my old cock. I fingered her slit. She had so much sperm in her. She stood up and sat on my lap. She had a tighter pussy, and now my old cock found pleasure here. She jumped on my cock while rubbing her own clitoris. My dick became stiffer now, and any moment sperm can squirt out. The feeling slowly grew stronger and yes, it came. I felt my dick tapping. It kept on bouncing. My dick was still hard, although it was starting to get numb. She whimpered as she kept bouncing. Eventually, she sat on top of me, slumped down. A grandmother came and pulled out my cock and did one last job. She sucked and licked all the sperm Everybody had their fun fucking. I went over to get my clothes that were left on the floor. On my black pants were a few drops of sperm stains. Someone must have fucked on my clothes.

Everyone had drunk the last round of wine before leaving. I was reminded to come back next Friday. Once in town, we split up and drove home in our own car.

I took a shower and spent the next hours thinking. What did I do? No doubt it was interesting to see someone's wife naked. Here we not only saw her naked, we touched her and fucked and locked ourselves in her pussy. Next Friday I was going to fuck this rossy coked-up granny's asshole. When I doggy fucked her, I saw her tight asshole.

AWESOME THREESOMES

"I'd like to try a threesome!" My wife's simple unsolicited one-liner about what had been an uneventful dinner at home up until that point caused quite a stir to say the least. Admittedly, as many husbands fantasize about it, I have been making this suggestion for years - and have been turned down with great hostility; so what happened? Was it something she had read, seen on television or in the cinema, or was it just a random thought that seemed fascinating? Honestly, I didn't care - if she was ready for it, so was I!!

Now the basic rules. After a series of lengthy discussions, we decided to have two independent events: a male-female-male and a male-female male-female. Each conversation was exciting and the anticipation was overwhelming. Oh dear, I was walking around half-erect all the time, and my wife was much more attentive in bed. Even if nothing more happened, it was already stimulating to just talk about it!

Before we present our game plan, let me describe both my wife and me. I am six feet tall, weigh 170 pounds, have brown eyes, black thinning hair, a 6-inch penis that is quite thick, and instead of having a six-pack for abs, my wife teases me by saying I have a one-pack. I have been an athlete all my life and have spent a reasonable amount of time at the gym. I am over 60 years old, but I don't look and act like one. Most people find me approachable, funny and "well-groomed".

My wife is gorgeously dead! She is 5'6" tall, weighs 110 pounds, has brown almond shaped eyes, reddish brown streaked hair, a sweet upturned nose, a great round and firm butt, fantastic thighs, hips and calves, perfect lips, silky skin and natural 34 Ds to die for. She also has a beautifully groomed pubic area with a pile of black pubic hair and is shaved from vagina to anus. She's younger than me and literally looks like she's in her 40s! We've been married since early college.

Once that was out of the way, the question arose as to where we would find willing partners. We thought of all sorts of places, but chose the most logical one - the gym. We both trained several times a week for several years and during this time we both found a number of friends and acquaintances. We decided to change our normal daily routine and to change and shower before and after each training session, still in the gym instead of at home. This would keep us with our friends a little longer and allow us to examine the "goods" more closely.

My wife determined what she would like a male partner to do, just as I did with the woman. The next week I spent time examining the 4 or 5 friends of mine that came into question. In the end I chose David for several reasons, he is: mid to late 40s, divorced, taller than me, very well built, has a solid ass and abs and has a very impressive "uncut" penis. In addition, David has made subtle remarks to me over the years about how beautiful my wife is and how lucky I am to be with her.

I turned to David and asked him if we could have a highly confidential conversation. When he agreed, I explained what we would ask of him, that this was a "one and done" and that there were no conditions. After assuring himself that I was serious, he declared his willingness to participate.

My wife had a similar experience in her dressing room. She approached both a blonde and a dark-haired woman - both beautiful and seductive. Both met my criteria: excellent body, fabulous face and lips, no tattoos or piercings, naturally large breasts and areolas and a well-cared for vagina. When she pointed this out to me, I decided to go for the dark-haired beauty - her name is Gabrielle, or Gabby for my wife.

My wife turned to Gabby, also in confidence, explained the same basic rules only once and pointed me to Gabby after the conversation so she could look at me. She liked what she saw and she agreed - our selection was now complete and on board.

The next phase of preparation was to figure out how we could do this. We came to the conclusion that there would be two different scenarios and that the male-female would be the first. We did this because we thought it was possible that David would not be as gentle as Gabby and that there might be some after-effects - like a sore pussy. So Gabby was invited to our home for a pleasant, relaxed evening, and later in the month David would join us in our dark, discreet and remote Italian trattoria.

The week's wait for the evening with Gabby seemed to go on forever. The anticipation for both my wife and me was really fun. We went through a series of scenarios, which in the end didn't matter because everything went smoothly. At 6pm Gabby arrived in a sun dress with spaghetti straps exposing her tanned shoulders and a pair of flat trousers. She looked beautiful. My wife was wearing black pants with a modestly low-cut white blouse and no bra. Me, khakis and a polo shirt.

My wife served hors d'oeuvres and we all started drinking a very good champagne while we got to know each other better. This lasted almost half an hour, then dinner was served together with more wine. As hoped, the wine began to work on both women, and the conversation revolved around sex and the reason why we were all together. More wine, and that was all that was needed. When my wife bent down to serve Gaby, she (Gaby) looked down at my wife's blouse, stretched her hand upwards, gently took my wife's neck and pulled it down to give her a soft, erotic and passionate kiss - with tongue. This was exactly the way my wife and I had hoped it would start. We quickly went

into the bedroom.

My wife made an excellent choice! Gabby is 50 years old, widowed for several years and has two teenage daughters living at home. She is six feet tall, weighs 120 pounds, has black hair, purple eyes and very fair skin. Like my wife, she has natural breasts, a C-cup, with large nipples that, when aroused, are pointed and straight outwards; very swollen pussy lips; she is firm and well-groomed - a product of a lot of yoga; and she has a bikini cut, which unfortunately for me has only left a "catwalk" of pubic hair (I like a bushier pussy). Shortly after going to bed we discovered that Gaby's most unusual body part is her clitoris: it is huge - much bigger than my wife. With no hair in that area, her clitoris is fully accessible and when she is aroused, incredibly sensitive. My wife and I were amazed and envious of her size and took turns touching, licking and sucking her. This was, I confess, a beautiful thing and a wonderful surprise!

Gabby and my wife undressed each other, then they both undressed me and led me to the bed. I was trapped between two beautiful women - unbelievable. The kissing and body contact started immediately. I had never had another woman since my marriage, and my wife had never been touched - let alone kissed - by another woman: This experience left us breathless at first. It was intoxicating. The girls kissed and touched each other's ears, neck, tits, pussy, ass and clitoris, while somehow they also paid a lot of attention to my body and penis. I can only describe the lovemaking of these two mature women as "refined" and very sensual. I paid that little bit to be the necessary man!

The first orgasm came quite quickly for each of us, then we engaged in a few wonderful hours of loving, touching, exploring, intercourse, cunnilingus and enjoying. The women all had multiple orgasms that seemed to never end and

I had 3. Around 1am we all showered together, got dressed and said good night. My wife and I agreed that this was even better than we could have imagined and we had another experience to look forward to.

After our first three-way conversation, our anticipation was heightened by the thought of the upcoming night with David. We met, as was fitting, at Amore's at 7 pm and went straight to our table. Speaking of fun: What I didn't know about this man was that he was both an excellent storyteller and had a wonderful sense of humor. We sat, drank, talked, drank some more and never mentioned why we were together. It was like an evening with a great, longtime friend.

After dinner my wife apologized to go to the bathroom and when she came back she leaned over the table and whispered so loudly that we could both hear that she wanted to go home. Then she told David that she had been watching him all night, looking forward to the rest of the evening, and that when she went into the ladies' room, she took off her panties because they were soaked and now the pussy juice was dripping down her leg!

That's all we wanted to hear! I paid the bill immediately and we all jumped into my car with my wife between the two men. Out of the corner of my eye I saw my wife take David's hand and let him stroke the inside of her silky smooth right thigh. She started moaning slightly, pulled up her skirt and let David stick his finger into her pussy - there was a conspicuous slurping sound and a wonderful smell that filled the car. I also noticed that my wife had reached over and rubbed against David's cock and squeezed it through his pants. My erection was palpable!

Once inside, my wife took total control. After she had asked us both to take off our clothes, she wanted David to stand behind her, unbutton her blouse and take off her bra without taking her breasts out of their cups, she just wanted the straps off her shoulders and her arms free. She asked me to kneel down before her, open her skirt, take off her shoes and gently kiss her clitoris while David cupped her breasts and let his erection rest in her ass crack. David and I did what she had been told to do.

Then my wife took a few steps to the side and turned back to us so that she was completely exposed and could watch the two men in front of her. What she saw must have pleased her, because the smile that fell on her face was something I had never seen before! David smiled as well. He and I were both standing in front of my naked wife with erections that could not get any bigger. We were all ready!

Our king-size bed offered just enough room for all of us to enjoy the evening. Since neither David nor I are bi, we both concentrated 100% on my wife. She was amazed at David's cock - it was a good 10 cm longer than mine, almost as thick and had a full hood, something she had never seen before even in pictures. What we did not do to her and she did not do to us!

We kissed, fucked and licked alternately her pussy and clitoris, also her anus, her toes, her wonderful tits, fingers, hands, ears, her neck. My wife screamed, squirmed and begged for more - we stroked her tits, face, hair and pussy - she had sperm dripping all over her body. It wasn't just sex, it was lust and it was intense.

She didn't miss most of our bodies either! My wife has a great head, and she demonstrated all her talents, she kissed and licked us all over our bodies, because she couldn't get enough of us or of her. She was so aroused that it felt like her mouth was literally devouring our faces and tails! I could only imagine it would be like this in an orgy. When I had an orgasm, she immediately turned to David to involve him and vice versa, while all the time she was having orgasms one after the other. Words cannot describe the evening - it was incredible, and my wife was incredible.

Like Gabby, when we were all used up, we showered together and my wife gave us both one last soapy hand job. Afterwards she fell into bed and fell asleep immediately; I took David home and thanked him. He asked when we could do it again, and after reminding him that it was a one-time occurrence, he said he was disappointed but understood.

Over the next few days, weeks, and months, my wife and I discussed the experiences at length as we relived our time with both David and Gabby. Our conclusion, which seems to change with every little nuance we remember, is that at the time of this writing, the evening with David was the winner - two cocks for my wife is much better than one. Apart from that our time with Gabby was unforgettable! Today I am not convinced that this will be our only "One and Done"!

CELEBDOM HOTEL

Hidden in a small corner of India, somewhere up in the Himalayas, is the Best Exotic Celebdom Hotel. Wrapped in the mists and secrets of the Himalayas, accessible only to its elite clientele of discrete celebrity females, the hotel offers a welcome retreat and a place to indulge in various nasty fetishes for various rich and powerful women.

The rules of the hotel are simple but binding, all participants must sign a waiver form and all participants must be consenting adults. Once on the hotel premises, women are the superior beings, friends or husbands accompanying each woman are considered to be strictly under the supervision of their mistresses. The hotel also provides a selection of their own slave men who are available to the celebrity clients. All these men are consenting adults who are accommodated in the hotel mainly for the money.

One of these slave boys is the recently selected Rex, tall, slim, with doe eyes, long hair, olive skin and beautiful lips. Rex is nineteen years old and, more importantly, he is a virgin. There was a massive bidding war for his services, which was eventually won by long-time member and Latina superstar Salma Hayek. And tonight she has arrived to claim her prize!

The priest presented himself naked and kneeling to Mrs. Hayek. Salma was impressed by what she saw, he was prettier in reality. She snapped her fingers and he crawled to her and submissively kissed her shoes, Rex had been trained for his first customer and he knew where his place was in this business.

"Take off my shoes and lick my feet, you beautiful puta boy," Salma said to him, Rex did what we were told, carefully took off her expensive shoes and licked the soles of the beautiful feet of his celebrity owner. Salma always basked in the power to make young, beautiful boys do nasty things for her, she slapped him in the face with her feet and shoved it in his mouth. Rex thanked her for the slap and began sucking her toes while making eye contact with his mistress, as he had been taught to do.

"Tonight, you are mine, so I can do what I want with you to satisfy my disgusting fetishes!

Rex couldn't believe that he was sharing such an intimate moment with a woman he had only seen in movies and on TV. Her hairy cunt was inches away, wet and glistening from her juices, and her spit was in his mouth - which actually helped to lubricate him as his mouth had become dry - and he had to lick her while she...

...a sound slap and a loud fart interrupted his reverie. "I'm not used to being kept waiting, bitch!" And Rex immediately started licking them. He put his chin on the seat, stuck out his tongue and tasted the salty wetness of his mistress, while her hair found its way into her mouth and nose, with Rex making sure to keep eye contact. Soon he heard two pops, and the backsplash hit his chin. Salma smiled with a strong smile and moaned lustfully while Rex's tongue worked its magic!

Rex knew that he was in love, he was now branded by Mistress Salma Hayek, and any future Mistress he might serve and marry would not only get a slave, but a celebrity who was branded and used by celebrities as a souvenir - Rex was so proud!

"I'm gonna hose the slave down, and I'm gonna pee, and I'm gonna drink it all, and I'm not gonna stop licking!"

And with the first sip of Salma's golden celebrity nectar, Rex himself arrived. And so Salma Hayek accepted Rex's submissive virginity!

THE HALLWAY

She arrived later than she had hoped and pulled into the parking lot, knowing that he was waiting for her. It was not the impression she really wanted to make, as if she was crawling for the first time, something he had described so eloquently that it haunted her mind for weeks. Quickly she ran to the door of a hallway between busy tourist shops that were just open and quite full and empty offices that were closed. She quickly walked down the dark corridor to the last room. He was in the dimly lit office, and when she came to the door, he took her bag and said, "Go back.

His simple two words instantly reminded her why she was there. She turned around without a word and went back until she heard him say stop.

"Get off" he said and she fell to her knees. He walked behind her, closed the door and turned on the light in the dark hallway. Her knees and hands felt the dirty carpet beneath them and she waited for Him to tell her what happened next.

She felt Him looking at her, but she did not look up at Him. She wasn't sure what the rules were and didn't want to find out the hard way, so she waited patiently for instructions. Her body was electrified while she waited.

"Pull up your skirt and pull out your tits."

She reached down and lifted the skirt of her short striped summer dress around her big round ass She was grateful that she had actually chosen to wear panties that day, because she kept thinking about the door and the busy main street, and if someone would go down and see her ass like that, what would it look like? A little voice told her she didn't care. Then she took her tits out of the top of her dress and left them hanging. She felt so exposed and still felt his eyes assessing her, not quite judging her, but judging her at the same time.

"Do you know there are shops on the other side of the door?" he asked as he walked down the long corridor back to his office.

"Yes, sir." She replied.

"Everyone could see her." He reminded her.

She looked up at him through her curly hair that was on her face and nodded. She watched him walk back down the hall and waited.

"Come." He just said. She felt the word in her heart, however, and began the long crawl down to Him. The sand on the carpet did not feel good on her knees, but she kept moving towards Him. She concentrated on making sure she did not stumble or hesitate. She knew she would get what she longed for when she made it down this hallway.

She crept past the door of the first store and was glad she didn't open. Then the second; she could almost hear the sounds of people as she swooped past with her DDs swinging at every move and her big ass in the air. The office door was getting closer and closer and He was standing there watching her and she kept moving towards Him and what He was offering her. She stood on His feet and He told her to go to the place.

She crawled further into the room to the mat that he had placed in front of a chair. She stayed on all fours in the dimly lit room that smelled of old books that were confusing her mind even more. Her knickers were soaked and she could feel them while she waited.

After the sound of the door closing, He came and stood beside her. The anticipation of what was to come made her tingle from head to toe. She saw the belt in His hand at His side and closed her eyes, took a breath and waited.

"Seven minutes," he said. "Seven minutes late. It's your first time, but we'll start with this."

The belt hit her covered ass. She inhaled sharply as the sting from the impact radiated. She felt it. She knew what she was in that moment; she knew why she was there.

"Well, go ahead, count up." He said.

Her body reacted to his words on an original level. "One." She said in a quiet voice as her panties got even wetter.

The leather belt hit her again, a little harder.

"Two," she said, taking a deep breath. Her mind cleared of everything but Him and what came next. She felt her nipples harden as she waited.

Again the leather clapped hard against her round ass while she stayed on all fours.

"On all fours." She said she flinched a little as the sting intensified. She closed her eyes and felt the pain, but realized she didn't like it. Her pussy hurt.

The sound of the leather hitting her ass broke the silence again. "Four." she said and moaned. She wasn't sure if she should enjoy it so much or if it was punishment for being late. Either way...

"Five." The sting intensified. Her bottom felt warm from the five hard strokes of his belt.

"Six." She gasped as one struck harder than any before, but she wanted more. She wondered if he was satisfied standing there watching her like that.

"Seven." She whimpered. The belt was on fire and she knew she was dripping. She waited in silence, on all fours, for his next command.

She felt his hands pull down her panties so he could see her naked ass. She was embarrassed, but wondered if her bottom had any marks. She felt the sting, the burning heat where the leather had hit her every time. She wondered if her butt looked good, but just when she thought about it, she felt his hand.

"Let's see how wet this made you." His fingers rubbed between her wet slits and slid gently along her pussy lips. She moaned as she felt his fingers inspect her.

"Mm hmm." She heard him say. "You're drenched." He said it very objectively. She felt her face blush as if a dirty secret was being revealed. Like his confirmation of her wet pussy would somehow tell the world what a hungry little bitch she was at that moment. She closed her eyes as he rubbed her, and moaned as he stopped. Her body longed for more - more of Him and she waited.

He got on the chair and sat down, his hard cock now in her face. She smiled. That was what she longed for at that moment, to taste Him and please Him. She knew this was what she was there for - His pleasure, but the belt had given her unexpected pleasure.

She felt her pussy hurt again when she felt the heat of the belt marks and saw His hard cock. She did not know how much she needed it until she had it.

"Go ahead and suck it," he said and leaned back in the chair to watch her

She remembered that he said he preferred no hands, so she stayed on all fours while she licked his cock. His hand held him so she could wrap her mouth around him. Slowly she slid her mouth down, her soft lips sliding down the length of his thick cock and trying to get it all the way down. She gagged herself with it, both because she knew he would like it and because she liked the challenge of getting as much as possible down her throat. She knew she was good at it and wanted to show him.

"Spread your legs a little wider," he said as she slowly moved her mouth up and down. "You know there's a mirror behind you."

She didn't know that and immediately felt nervous, afraid the view wasn't good enough, but also knew that hopefully she wouldn't bother him with the mirror if she kept gagging her slutty little mouth against his cock. She was hungry for it and focused on how it felt in her mouth, trying to forget what he said about the mirror while continuing to feel the sting of the belt.

His cock felt good as it slid between her lips and she loved how thick it was when she sucked it down. Her mouth bobbed up and down on it, picking up the pace and trying her best to suck it well. She heard him moan and continued.

"That's it." He said. His words made her pussy tingle and made her suck a little faster. Deeper. Her mouth was full of saliva running down her chin. Her face got messy as she lost her way and sucked His amazing cock. She let her drool slide down her chin to the floor and no longer cared what she looked like. She wanted to taste it. She wanted to hear His moaning as it came into her mouth. That was all she could think about at that moment.

She gagged herself deep on his cock again. The saliva came out as she choked on his cock. "That's it." He said softly and encouraged her to keep doing what she was doing.

She pulled back and went straight down again, chin covered with spit, and gagged herself even tighter on his cock. Her saliva almost came out of her nose, her eyes watering. She didn't care what she looked like. As soon as she heard his voice again, she knew she was on the verge of getting what she longed for. "That was it. Just like that," he said.

She didn't care that her knees hurt because she was on all fours. She didn't care that she looked like a sloppy mess. She only had one job: to suck his cock. She bounced her head up and down on his cock and soon felt his hands on both sides of her head. His moaning became more frequent. She sucked harder and wanted to taste it. He grunted and she went deep on his cock and felt the first strand of sperm shoot into her throat. It made her pussy drip as she swallowed it. His cock pulsated between her lips and she kept it as deep as she could and made it flow into her throat like the little cock-sucking bitch that she was. She pulled away a little and tasted him. His sperm on her tongue, her reward for a job well done. She moaned with His cock in her mouth and kept swallowing His semen until every last drop was in her belly, as befits a good girl.

LAZY MORNING

I turn around this morning and look in your direction. You are sleeping soundly and peacefully. The sheet that barely covers your belly button moves slowly up and down with each breath. inwards. Out. On. Off. God, I could watch you forever. But there's too much cover-up for my taste.

I'll reach over gently so as not to wake you. I don't want to ruin this moment. You're relaxed and carefree. Your face is smooth and your lips are slightly pursed. I gently lift the sheet and slide it down your legs. It's warm in here (or is it just me).

Oh dear, I always wake up horny. Every morning. Your cock is naked and lies on your inner thigh. My hand twitches as I try to hold it back. I want to touch the soft, silky skin. Lightly, so easily I pull my fingertips over you. I listen attentively to your breathing. I feel that I have to catch my breath.

Your cock twitches a little if you open your legs wider. Unconsciously I welcome my playfulness. You move a little in my direction. Mmmmmmm! Much better! My fingers are working their way down to your balls. I take them in my hands and rub them gently.

I lay my tongue flat and stroke with my lap from your body outwards and cover your balls. My left hand rests on your right ass cheek. When my licking excites me, I squeeze. My right hand gently strokes your cock. My tongue scurries back into my mouth to collect more saliva for the next lick.

After paying special attention to your balls, my eyes are drawn to your semi-hard cock. Damn, that looks good. All set for me. My mouth is watering and I'm licking my lips. Your body is too tempting. I have to try hard to let you sleep as long as possible. I enjoy having fun with you so much.

I slowly glide closer to your cock. My eyes on your face test my alertness. You are still peacefully motionless. I lower my head and reluctantly blow hot air over your shaft. I look up at your face. The side of your mouth has bent a little upwards, but your body lies loosely in sleep.

I moisten my tongue and slightly feel the head of your cock. Slowly I circle. I enjoy the feeling of you on my tongue. You grow as I watch. You grow longer and wider. Your body prepares for me. My mouth waters more. I move my tongue back and forth along your shaft.

Finally, I can't go on. I suck the head of your cock into my mouth. I continue sucking and start swirling my tongue around. I love the feeling of your hard cock in my mouth. I put my left hand so that it gently surrounds your balls and rubs them lightly.

My breathing becomes a little irregular. I feel the wetness between my legs. I'm so fucking turned on that your cock in my mouth is getting hard. The taste and feel of you going in and out of my mouth is so exciting!

I notice a cramp in your breath and look up to see you watching me attentively. Your eyes seem to sparkle a little while you smile sleepily down at me. Shit! I know that look, and I can hardly wait for the pleasure that comes with it.

Without words, I start sucking a little more. Hollowing out my cheeks and twirling your beautiful cock. My left hand continues to gently caress your balls while my right hand grabs your ass. I keep my eyes on yours because I know how much you love to see the desire in my eyes as you watch your cock and my mouth.

You grab my hips and pull them towards your head. Your hand starts rubbing my ass. I squirm at the light touch. My wetness begins to run down my thigh. When you feel it, you move your hand towards my pussy. You're smearing my juices all over my pussy lips. So fucking wet.

This time you're gonna grab my hips a little bit roughly and pull one leg over your head. You lift your head up and pull the tip of your tongue over my pussy lips. I hear a growl deep in your throat. Holy shit. This is gonna be good.

Your tongue dives into my pussy and fucks me over and over again. It feels so fucking good. I'm trying to concentrate on your cock, which I'm frantically sucking right now. The tip of your tongue starts circling my clit. You flick back and forth. Faster. Fuck! I look down to see that I've somehow swallowed most of your hard cock. I feel my orgasm. It's almost there. Fuck, yeah! Please!!!

I take a deep breath and lower my head completely and suck with everything I've got. You nibble on my clitoris and I break screaming around your dick. Then you come and grunt. Your head is still between my legs. Your tongue licking the sperm dripping from my pussy. I swallow as much of your sperm as I can before I let it drip down your cock.

I lick up your sperm and turn around to smile at you. Good morning, baby!

ANGRY FUCK

I'm so fucking angry! The jerk's at it again. What the hell was he thinking? I'm gonna beat his ass! Turn him into a bloody pool at my feet. I implore the universe to send him to me today, NOW! If I think about it too long, I might kill the son of a bitch.

I hear the door open, and I'm ready to strike. Click. The asshole comes in. I pull out and punch him in his smug face. Asshole! He jumps back a bit with a stupid look on his face. (laughs) Ha! It takes him a second to figure out what's going on. This could be my chance. I start crying on him with everything I got. My fists are clenched so tight, the nails are biting my palms. The stupid jackass is built, but I'm hoping to do some damage. He doesn't even bother to block my punches.

He pushes me against the wall with his back and puts his hands over my head. Holy shit! I think he's had enough. He comes closer and tries to kiss me, and I kick as hard as I can against his legs, still trying to confuse him. Not good. He's much bigger and stronger than me. It seems I'm not making any progress. I might as well try moving the whole apartment building.

He pushes me against the wall, his body pressed firmly against mine. His dick is hard as ever. He's breathing a little hard. HA! This seems to be my only victory, albeit a small one. In one quick movement he backs away, turns me around and presses my chest against the wall.

My tits are pressed flat. My nipples hurt. His feet push mine roughly apart. "Behave yourself!" He whispers in my ear. His hand reaches around me and feels my pussy through my shorts. I fight to get away. How humiliating that he finds out so easily that I'm aroused. Goddamn it! I have to get him off me. He slides his hand under my shorts and underwear right onto the part of my body that always seems to betray me.

I hate the smug laugh that barks in my ear. No matter how angry I am, just one touch from him and my juices take full effect. When he pinches my clitoris, I can't stop my moaning. Another laugh. To hell with him! He forces his fingers into me with little resistance. His fingers pump relentlessly into me. Then they are gone.

He sucks each finger into his mouth one by one, licking and slurping loudly on my wetness. What an ass! With one hand he lets go of his rock-hard cock and strokes it several times. Then he pushes my clothes under my waist.

With his fingers he explores my asshole. He turns in circles and drives me crazy. Now he plays with me. He gives in a little when he knows what I need. Caresses me lightly when I need a hard fuck. If he doesn't do it soon, I'll... Oh shit, I ain't gonna do nothing. There's not a fucking thing I can do. The way my hands are tied, I'm at his mercy. He'll take me when he's good and ready. I give up, knowing that's what I want anyway. I stop fighting it and my body loosens in his grip.

He lets go of my hands, but I hold them against the wall for him. This hand comes around to tease my nipples while he goes on with my butt. I am so close to breaking. If he could just touch me a little harder. I spread my legs wider, hoping he'll take pity on me.

I feel his throbbing dick head bang my asshole. Fuck! My body cramps up, throbbing as he comes in. I fucking hate him, but I want him so bad, my body hurts when he's not inside me. He rams the rest of his huge cock up my ass, up to my balls. Yeah! Yeah! Please! This is what I need. He's yelling at me. That big pole is slapping my poor ass. SMACK! Oh yeah! Son of a bitch! I fucking hate you! In and out. Holy shit, that feels so fucking good! No, wait, I wasn't gonna back down this time. SMACK! Mmmmm, that hurt.

His teeth seem to pierce the tender flesh between my neck and shoulder while I scream my joy/hate / ecstasy / pain / love from the top of my lungs. His cock twitches as he shoots something that feels like gallons of cum to soothe my decimated ass. I'm closing the shutter. No power. Carried to sleep by the focus of my entire being. The one who will continue to use me as he sees fit.

ADULTS MAKING OUT

So the thrill of the unknown. The romance-reading virgin who wonders about the things she's read about. The kiss is pretty important. He can make or break a deal. Trying out interesting men. Finding the one who makes your toes curl and your back arch.

Kisses, of course, quickly lead to violent caresses over clothing. Clothed bodies touch each other timidly at first. Light exploratory touches. Grabbing his butt through the soft jeans that caught my eye at first.

Squeezing bodies together. I feel his hard cock pressing into my leg. Squirming. The pain between my legs gets worse. Grinding harder against that hard cock. Will it look like the ones I've been looking at in the dirty magazines my friend hid?

I'm getting braver. The need for more drives me on. My hand on his knee as he kisses my neck. Chills run through my body. Slowly I pull my hand up his leg to 'accidentally' brush his hardness. His moaning. My gasping. Does it get better than that?

As if his hand is creeping under my shirt in response. It's working its way up to my breasts. He squeezes it tight through my bra. My nipples are pebbling and my back is arching. "Are you okay, baby?" is whispered in my ear.

The smothered moan of my spread lips immediately followed with a "Yes, please." The cups of my bra are lowered. His hands brush my hellishly hard nipples. Damn, his rough fingertips feel heavenly. "Don't stop." streams from my lips. "Need more" moans softly in his ear.

My shirt was lifting. Will he like my breasts? I look down at myself and then up at him. His eyes were on my chest. He seems to pause forever. Very slowly he lowers his head. Gently he kisses my right nipple while his right hand continues to caress my left breast.

With his tongue popping out, he plunges down onto my nipple. He slowly sucks it into his mouth and seems to growl deep in his throat. The vibration tickles my skin. While he pinches the tip, a sharp pleasure seems to connect my nipples with my clitoris and my pussy. I squeal and wriggle around, causing another moan from him.

He changes breasts. He gives both of them the same attention. My nipples get even more wet from his saliva pebbles when he pulls away to blow on them. He pushes me on my back and adjusts to where he is between my legs.

Shit. I can feel his hard cock against my clitoris. His body has caused my legs to spread. Also, my pussy lips split and leave me open to the wonderful pressure while he rubs against me. His hips rock and let me feel his hardness sliding back and forth on my clitoris.

I am now also disgusting. I can no longer calm down. I want the constant pressure and friction. I can feel my underwear getting wet. I tell him how much I love it when he lets me go like this. Tell him how good it feels and beg him to let me cum.

I have entered a world that feels like an alternative world. One where I'm so turned on I'm not able to be conscious of myself. A place where only my feelings and his feelings count. I drag myself back into it. I turn my hips so that he touches me exactly where I need him to.

"Please, baby, let me cum", I beg him in my desperate need to grab his back. At this moment I would do almost anything. He stops and pulls back a little bit. I whimper about the loss.

"Don't be sad, baby. You'll feel really good," he promises me. "Be patient."

His hands move to my pants button. He stops and looks up at me questioningly. I nod my head excitedly to see if his hands will feel as good as mine. His fingers seem to tremble a little as he releases the button. Slowly he pushes open the zipper.

Butterflies are dancing in my stomach. I have waited so long for his touch. I am nervous and excited at the same time. His lips find mine again while he gently slides his hand between my underpants and my belly. I giggle a little. He watches my eyes closely while his fingers split my pussy lips. He pauses to see if I'm going to protest or tense up.

The tip of his finger hardly touches my clitoris and my hips jerk. I laugh out loud and grab his head to kiss him harder. I gather my bravery to show him that I am ready. I lower my hand into his lap and begin to rub my hand over his swollen cock. I love the feeling he has under his jeans.

He starts rubbing me slowly and sucks on each nipple in turn. After I open his jeans I slide my hand down his belly and into his pants. My eyes are on his all the time to see how he reacts. When my palm touches his cock and I grab him, I close his eyes and he moans right into my ear. The combination of all these things causes a cramp in my pussy. The feeling of soft skin over steel, the sounds he makes and his fingers rubbing against my clitoris all together cause my ruin.

My body arches towards his. My hand pumps his cock faster than my body begins to break. His fingers do not stand still. I feel like I'm losing my mind. I try to get away from that feeling. It's almost too much.

He won't let me move away. I curse and beg when my second orgasm hits me. I scream, my body shakes. I have lost all sense of time and space. My head feels spacious and my body tingles and is hypersensitive. When I look down, I see wetness on the front of his jeans and feel satisfied to curl up in his arms and rest.

THE FIRST MEETING

We've been sending messages for weeks. We exchange thoughts and sometimes discuss things that bend my toes. Finally it was decided that we had to see if there was something between us personally.

We agreed to meet far away from our two houses in a nice hotel. I was to arrive there first. I take a long, relaxing bath without touching myself, as ordered. I dry off and crawl into the middle of the big bed.

I put the thick, black blindfold over my head and lie back. I relax. I spread my legs towards the lower corners of the bed.

My body immediately reacts to the cold in the air. I fight against the instinct to cover myself, raise my arms and cross them over my head. And wait. . .

Will you come now? I try to distract myself with thoughts of what you might do to me. The air in the room makes my nipples hurt so much it hurts. From time to time I feel a cool breeze on my warm pussy.

Oh shit, can I take that with me? Yes. This is what I wanted. What I asked you for. The waiting. . .

...CLICKING. The door opens. God, I hope it's you. I don't know how else to explain it. Could I be protecting myself if it was someone else?

A growl I got addicted to comes from the direction of the door. Then silence. A whisper in my ear, "Good girl." At the jerk that makes my pussy squeeze, I squeeze my legs. Her stern voice beside me orders me to open my legs.

God, I can already feel the juices dripping down my ass. They haven't even touched me yet, and I'm almost gasping.

The bottom of the bed plunges in. Your strong hands are pushing my legs further apart. I can hear your inhalation, but I have no idea what you're doing. Then a warm puff of air on my overheated sex.

Another growl makes my body firmer again. Don't move, just your breath. I tremble when it hits my flowing juices and cools them on my skin. "Mmmmm. You smell delicious," you growl. "My good girl is already dripping for me."

I flinch when I feel your warm tongue licking from my ass to my clit. Oh, fuck! "What a sweet, wet pussy."

I whimper.

You slowly crawl up my body and lay your clothed body on top of mine. Your tongue caresses my lower lip. Mine stretches out to wriggle with yours. You're right. I do taste good.

I put my arms around your neck and want to taste more of me on your tongue, but they are raised above my head again. "Uh-uh, baby girl. I like you right where you were. I'll give you what you need. Wait for my instructions before you move."

God, I want to move my hands up and down on your body. I can't see. I keep having this nice feeling you get when you stretch really well. My body stretches under yours.

Your shirt scraping across my hard nipples is driving me crazy. Your hard cock pressing against my open pussy lips is sweet torture.

Part of me wants to turn you over, pull your dick out and ride it all I want. The other part wants to be taken care of, so I wait.

You seem to understand that I'm gaining control of myself. You say "good girl" and start licking, nibbling and kissing you from my mouth to your neck. Your tongue and mouth feel so hot and wet. You lick slowly and thoughtfully.

When you move down, you stop. "I want you to arch your back so I can taste those sexy tits... There you go. That's it. Mmmmm."

I feel like shock waves are traveling from my nipples to my clit. When you lick one, lightly stroke your hand over the other.

Holy shit. I feel like my body could explode into a million tiny pieces at any moment. Please, for the love of God, I need some relief. "Please," I whisper.

"All in good time, you greedy girl." You growl. "I'll fuck you, but you'll have to wait." With that, the wonderful pressure of your weight on my body disappears.

Holy shit. What have I done? God, I just want to do what you want me to do. It's so fucking hard to lie still while you take your time with my overwrought body.

My wheezing's starting to slow down. I'm trying to listen to anything that might give me a clue as to what you're doing. Nothing at first. Then a slight rustle and a slow zip. Relief washes over me that you didn't leave me.

After what seems like an eternity, I hear you coming my way. "Okay, greedy girl. I'm gonna put you up. You will sit exactly as I sit you down. Understand?" rumbles out of your mouth.

"Yes, sir" comes automatically out of mine. Your strong hands will slowly set me down, legs away from the edge of the bed. I'm so glad you left slowly. If I was blindfolded, I'd have freaked out if I'd been dragged upright.

You take my hands and put them on your hips. l "II give you two minutes to use your hands. You waited so patiently. Go ahead, don "t be shy now. The clock is ticking."

There's so much I want to touch, but so little time. I reach up and lightly touch your breast. Oh, dear. The smoothness of your skin is delightful. I can feel the definition in your chest and your stomach. You certainly do take care of your body. My hands begin to tremble in my excitement.

I reach around to grab your behind. Firm but juicy. Mmmmm! "One minute". I move quickly to your crotch where I find the answer to whether you are also aroused. God, it's so hard. The soft, silky skin of your dick slides under my hands. Your cock twitches when I lick my lips.

"Patience, little one." I'm stroking your cock as I slowly enjoy the feeling of it sliding between my hands. I rub the tip of your cock and find it wet. I move one hand to cupping your balls while I bring the other to your mouth.

The salty taste sends shivers down my spine. "Did you like the little one?" You ask. I shake my head. "Say it. I enjoy hearing your voice and I want you to answer me fully," you command.

Holy shit. I love it when you get demanding. I force the words out in a whisper. "Yes, sir. I love the taste of your salty sperm in my mouth."

You start laughing with that greeting. Oh, what a beautiful sound. "There may be hope for my shy girl after all." The sound of your deep, guttural laughter is causing my cooch to cramp. I like making you happy. I like it a lot.

"Your two minutes are up. Put your hands behind your back. That's it, just on your little back. Mmmm! I love the way it makes your tits pop out." Your praise makes me cringe. "Cold kitty?" you growl. "Let's see what I can do to make you warmer."

The musky scent of your excitement grows stronger. I take it deep into my lungs. Every time I think I'm as horny as I can be, you do something to make it stronger.

"Open that pretty mouth and stick out your tongue." My tongue sticks it out right now. "Good girl. Now I'm going to give you instructions. Let's see how well you can follow them. Don't do anything unless you're told to." moans your stern voice.

The silky wet tip of your cock traces my lips. Instinctively, I lick my lips. Your bark scares me. "No! Not until you're told! Stay very still." My nipples get pinched and released.

My eyes are watering behind my blindfold. I want to be good. This time I feel the soft, smooth skin on the side of your cock rubbing my right cheek. I am holding still. I'm waiting. "I will now place my big, hard cock near your mouth. I want you to start at the head and slowly lick your way down my shaft."

"Yes, sir." I'm panting softly. I've been waiting for this for what seems like an eternity. My heart is pounding while my tongue eagerly swishes to and fro at the tip of your cock. I lick a couple of times before I ask, "Like this?"

"Yes, sweet girl. Just like that. Keep going." The salty taste makes my mouth water. God, I want to suck you into my mouth.

My body's shaking because I want you now. I force myself to quietly take what I'm given. I'm licking and kissing down on each side. I'm waiting. "That felt wonderful, little one. Next, I want you to suck the head of my cock any way you want."

I'll take the end of your dick in my mouth and suck it, hollowing out my cheeks, my tongue twirling around the edge. I want as much of your cock as I can get. My mouth is watering.

Your moaning and growling is heavenly. You keep my pussy soaking wet. I feel a hand on the back of my head just before you start pumping your hips slowly. "So warm and wet. I'm gonna fuck your mouth now, pretty girl. Is that what you want?"

"Uh huh" I'm drooling around your dick.

"Tell me!" Your voice clatters. You pull back and let me speak.

"Yes, please."

"No, I said tell me! Ask for what you want. Speak up, so I can hear everything you say." You're gasping for air.

I summon up all my courage and burst: "Please use my mouth. I want you to fuck him good. I love the taste of your sexy, hard cock." You cut me off by doing exactly that. Your jabs hit me in the back of the throat.

"Get him! Relax your throat." You hold the end of your dick against the back of my throat until I choke. You pull back. Drool runs down my chin and down your dick. "Good girl." Your voice catches.

"One more time." Your cock chokes me again. It scares me a little, but not because I think you're going to hurt me. I just don't want to disappoint you. I'm choking again, hoping my spit and drool won't break anything.

"What a beautiful mouth that takes my huge cock. I love watching it disappear into your hot, wet mouth." You keep praising me and moaning as you stomp in and out of my mouth.

I lose track of time. All I know is that thick shaft that pumps in and out. Until it disappears and I moan and groan. "Now it's my turn." You're choking.

"I want your head on the bed and your beautiful ass in the air. Your legs spread." You just put me down like this and step away. "Little girl, your legs are covered. Your sweet pussy is dripping wet."

Again your tongue licks my pussy lips and collects the juices that ooze out of it. I arch my back so you lick my clit.

Again with the sexy laugh. It's a bit of a snarl and giggle at the same time. My pussy's cramping up again. "Does my laughter turn you on, little girl? Do you like making me happy? What a good girl you are," you say.

I smile proudly. Then you stick your tongue deep into my cunt. Your face buried in my soaking wet pussy. Your tongue, licking wildly inside me, driving me crazy.

There's that snarling sound coming from your throat again. Shit, you sound like a wild animal. Instead of being afraid, it just pushes me closer. Holy shit. It feels so good to have you inside me.

"Please!" I scream.

"Please what, my sweet-tasting girl?" You ask. I am so confused right now. I just want to come so damn much. "Please suck on your clit?" you say, lowering your face back to my aching clit and sucking it hard into your mouth.

"Fuck!" I moaned.

"Or please bury my big fucking dick balls deep inside that tacky pussy," you ask while ramming two fingers into me. Holy shit, I start to contract, but then your fingers are gone.

"Please let me cum. I need to cum so bad." I'm sobbing.

I arch my back and open my legs as wide as I can. I don't care what comes next, because I know you'll take care of me.

You're gonna pull my hips towards you and enter in one long, slow motion. "Do you like my throbbing cock inside of you?" you ask as you walk out with your butt on the outside and stop. Your balls rub against my clitoris and send shivers down my whole body. "Answer me! Is that what you want?" you start to slowly pull out of my trembling body.

"No! Please fuck me hard! Please fuck me as hard as you want." I beg you. Besides, you're starting to pick up speed. I think I'm about to get it.

"Well, guess what. I'm not ready for you to come." You take a break. "How are you feeling, little girl?" you ask, pushing in and out of me at a leisurely pace.

"I feel like I'm going crazy! Please make me come, damn it!" Tears are running down my eyes. "It feels too good. I can't stand it any longer," I say.

"Oh, sweet girl, you can and you will take what I give you. However I choose to give it to you." You say, punctuated by moans and lamentations from both of us, while your cock maintains its torturous pace.

You maintain this pace for hours, which seems like hours. Every time I get close and think it's time, you slow down or stop.

At first, I try to fight it, but eventually I give in and just lie there with the feeling. I feel your hard cock moving back and forth. The cool air is blowing over my sweat and juice-soaked body. I hear all the beautiful noises you make when you enjoy my pussy wrapped tightly around your cock. I hear the dirty words grunting and growling while you also hold back. I hear the noises my pussy makes when you slide through her wetness.

My breath is coming in my pants now. I'm a little euphoric. I'm thankful now for everything you give me. I sigh.

"Okay, little one. Now you're ready." You grunt. You grab my hip with one hand and my hair with the other. "I want you to come now. I want you to get ready." ...rumbling from your throat. And your hips start pounding into mine.

"Holy shit! Fuck, yeah! Oh, God, yes. Please. Fuck!" I scream while your cock smashes into my sore pussy.

"Sperm on my fucking dick! I want you to pour it in my legs. Fucking do it! Hose down now! NOW, GODDAMN IT!" My body's splintering. It's cramping really fucking hard over and over again. My pussy squirts its juices all over your cock, legs and even a little bit up your belly.

In the distance, I can hear you roar. "Fuck yeah, soak me! You're fucking squeezing my dick so fucking hard. You pull it out and shoot your cum all over my back and ass. It's so fucking warm on my sweat-soaked skin. I feel myself getting lowered and covered over on the bed as I drift off into unconsciousness. My last thought is that I can't wait to see what tomorrow will bring.

HAPPY HALLOWEEN

I wake up from a Halloween nap feeling a little weird. It's normal for me to wake up feeling horny. But today I also feel a tension in the air that I have never noticed before. There is a dreamlike haze around everything.

I shake it off and decide to prepare myself for the trick-or-treat. I go to my closet to get the cute new outfit I just bought. Where the hell is it? In its place is a dirty-looking tunic and metal cuffs. What the hell is going on here?

Never mind. I can roll with this. Maybe I'm still asleep. There's a note on the new costume that says, "Wear this to trick-or-treat. I'm a little old for this, but I think it's a joke. Let's do it.

I'll put the costume over my head. The fabric is scratching my soft skin. I put the collar on. Then I move to each wrist. When they snap shut, a strange feeling comes over me. A bit like panic. It's a costume. Why am I freaking out? I giggle a little. I can take it off anytime I want.

As I try, I realize I can't. I keep putting on all three and freaking out more and more. They won't let me take them fucking off. My panic is interrupted by the ringing at my door. I run to get it, hoping that whoever it is can help me.

The door opens and I look inside a naked chest. I look up at the man's face. It's free of any feeling. I'm so startled. He grabs my shackles and pulls me out the door. He leads me to my neighbor's house. Thank God I can get help there.

We reach the door and I ring the bell. It opens, but I don't recognize the thing when I turn around. It's certainly not my neighbour. "Trick-or-treat"? I'm not sure what's going on.

There's something in front of me with red skin and horns. As his mouth opens, I notice rows of sharp teeth. They remind me of the mouth of a shark. Fuck. I'm in trouble.

"Come, slave!" comes a growl from the thing's dangerous mouth. Everything inside me tells me to run away. It drags me into a room with no furniture. "Get on your knees!" Immediately I fall to my knees. "Stop!" What am I, a fucking dog?

He leaves the room. Now it's time to run, but I can't seem to move from my kneeling position. I look around and try to find a way out. I'm trying to find a way out. I can't see anything.

That red, demon-looking thing is coming in. It's obviously a male, because he has his huge red cock in his hand and he's stroking it. He runs after me and keeps stroking it. I hear the sound of his hands slowly sliding back and forth. What has he planned?

After a seemingly eternal time, the demon walks in front of me. "Open!" he commands. He puts his hand on my jaw and squeezes it so my mouth does what he wants. "Now! You will do it well, or I promise you your trick," he says with a grin that resembles a grin.

I open my mouth as wide as I can. His penis is damn big. I'm terribly afraid that I won't be able to do it. He grabs the back of my head and forces my head towards him. His cock is filling my mouth. The head is on my throat before I'm ready.

I choke. My mouth and my eyes are watering. He moans. He sends a moan to my nipples. They tense to the point of discomfort and rub against the rough fabric of my clothes. I whimper.

I reach up and try to exert some kind of control. He growls at me. "No! Take it as a slave." He's pulled out the farthest before he moves quickly back so I have to gag again. He speeds up and fucks me in the face. I hold still and suck as hard as I can.

His moaning with pleasure makes my pussy wet. I have tears and spit dripping in my face while my juices run down my leg and onto the floor.

The demon screams, and I have a flood of semen in my mouth. I swallow and swallow, but it still oozes out of my mouth. It falls to the ground to join my juices. My pussy cramps up and my body starts shaking.

He's done and pulls his cock out. My jaw is sore and my body is still aching for release. The demon grabs my neck cuff and takes me back to his front door. My escort from earlier is waiting there.

I am driven to the next house. My body is still tingling. I have semen on my chin and on my outfit. I am in a strange state and my appearance does not bother me.

At the next door I ring the bell again. It opens and I enter. I wait for instructions. The thing that greets me looks half animal and half human. Again the man parts are huge and the cock is so hard. He bends down and licks me from chin to forehead. A soft growl is heard just before he grabs the neck of my tunic and pulls it down to my belly button. My perky nipples are no longer hidden. His brute force makes me pant.

His tongue starts to lick again. First my neck, where he nibbles and nibbles. Then he goes deeper. His tongue nibbles at my right nipple. He sucks it into his mouth. I can feel it in my cunt. Oh, fuck so good.

He goes on to the other titty licking, sucking and growling. He reaches down and his hand pushes up the bottom of my tunic. His fingers dip into my pussy and come out soaking wet. He wraps his fist around his cock and spreads my juices all over his cock.

He puts his thick cock between my soft tits and starts moving his hips. At first slowly but quickly he gains speed and grunts and moans loudly. His fingertips maintain the constant friction on my nipples while he fucks my tits.

Just as I feel my body coil up to release, he takes his cock in his palm and brings it to my mouth. He growls and unleashes his cum all over my face and on my tits. My pussy cramps up again, but again no relaxation. Motherfucker.

I stick out my tongue to taste more of his sperm. Mmmmmm. My hands rub it into my chest. I bring my fingers to my mouth and I clean them one by one. Again, I am led to the door.

This time I leave without being led to the next house. I ring the bell and wait for my "trick or treat". I cannot quite decide which one it is. My body is so aroused, but there seems to be no release for me.

As I am led through my street to each house, the things I encounter are different. What they do to me is different. What is the same thing you might think? Well, in every single house, I am pushed to the edge without any relief.

I'm being taken back to my house. Where all this madness began. I think it's over now. The door opens and I kick in. Why is my escort following me inside? Then I understand. All the creatures I visited tonight have gathered at my house.

I am picked up, stripped and placed on my kitchen table. The demon comes to stand next to my head and says, "Good slave. Now it's your turn." Then he pulls on my body so that my head hangs off the side of the table.

His dick is on my mouth. He pushes his way in. While he's slowly fucking my mouth, I can take the time to lick and suck his beautiful cock. I enjoy the length he pushes himself down my throat. I love the width that expands my mouth wide. In and out he continues his slow pace.

I begin to notice that the others who were watching are now touching me. My tunic has been torn from my body and I am lying there completely naked so that everyone can see it. The demon nods his head and growls. Everyone around me begins to lick, pull, pinch, rub and suck every inch of my body.

I feel a mouth on each nipple. The sucking makes me crawl on the table. My body bows as mouths and fingers alternately fuck my soaked pussy.

My demon lover has withdrawn from my mouth and is going to the other end of the table. He straightens his big red dick. I wait for him to ram it all the way up. Instead, he slowly comes into my needy hole. It feels like he never goes down. He's so slow.

I need him hard and fast. Why is he doing that? I whimper. Finally he's got his dick all up in me. He bends over me, comes right into my ear and growls "NOW!!".

My whole body seems to be shattering. I'm floating in a haze of lust. As my pussy locks like a vice, he starts pumping inside me. "No, no, no, no, no, no!" I sing. I can't go on.

No one listens to me. The demon continues to pound on my pussy with jackhammers like punches. I'll scream when I come back. Everyone's holding me now. My body wants to move, but it can't.

The demon screams and the sperm fills my pussy. It's too much for me to hold on to and it's pouring down my legs. Everyone else starts licking everything. My mind has reached its limit and I pass out.

When I wake up, I realize that I'm lying in bed. I stretch out and get out of bed. I take a shower and get dressed. It's time for my morning walk.

Last night I had the strangest hot dream ever. I must have splashed in my sleep because my body is well saturated and I actually feel like I've been fucked. What a fucked-up dream.

The neighbours are being extremely friendly this morning. What the fuck is going on? Everyone greets me and looks at me with a strange look. They grin and look at me more than usual.

I am almost home when I see a hot man coming out of the house next to mine. He goes to the mailbox and pauses. I slow down to pass him. I need a better look. As I pass him, he steps forward, leans towards me and growls in my ear. I come fast and hard. Happy Halloween!!

MY NEIGHBOR'S FIRST VISIT

I'll meet you in the lobby of our apartment building. You are sexy with the body of a god. Yummy! I'm too shy to say anything, but you ask if I want to have a drink with you. We sit in the common area and have a few glasses of wine before we decide to spend the night.

You accompany me to my room and give me a quick kiss. "I enjoyed our conversation. See you later," you say.

I just giggle nervously. I know what you're thinking, but the thoughts that go through my mind are anything but childish.

I go to my apartment and get naked for the bed. My nipples ache from the excitement of the night. I will never fall asleep unless I jerk off to relieve the tension you have brought to my body.

I lie down and lightly brush my firm nipples as I think of you. It tingles all the way down to my pussy. My body tightens with the feeling as I continue stroking.

I wonder what your mouth would feel like against my aching nipples. I begin to track my clitoris with the tip of my finger. That kiss was amazing. If I'd been a brave girl, I would have pulled you into my room

There's a knock at my door. Who the hell is it? It's late, so I'm ignoring it. It's knocking a little louder again. Goddamn it! I'm trying to jerk off and some idiot knocks on my door. I put on a bathrobe and march off to see who I'm fucking.

When I open the door, you rush in. You close and lock the door before pushing me against the wall. "Yeah, so now it's later. I've forgotten something," you pant in my face. "I forgot that."

With these words you press your body against mine and kiss me like an animal. My mouth and neck are attacked. I'm shocked that I'm seriously aroused.

"Please" slips out of my mouth as you devour me.

You push my robe to the floor and step back. Thank God there's a wall or I'd be a pile on the floor.

"Spread your damn legs!" you ask. I can feel my pussy bubbling as I wait to see what you're gonna do. "You smell like sex. I just fucking left. What did you do?" you ask.

I sort of stutter "touch myself" and look down embarrassed.

You touch my hands and smell them both until you find the fingers that were just tracing my clitoris. "Mmmmmm! They smell delicious. Don't stop on my account." You sit down with this.

"Wwww-what?" I wonder if I fell down a rabbit hole. That shit doesn't happen to me. Then it hits me. I'm dreaming. Then fuck it, let's do it.

My hands are moving back to their previous positions. My left hand gently brushes my nipple. My right hand grabs the moisture between my legs. After I find it, I stroke my clitoris and gently spread my juices on it to make it nice and smooth.

I place my foot on the windowsill right next to you. It feels wonderful because I have opened up so you can see how swollen my needy clitoris is. My fingers keep circling. "Damn, that feels so good!" I moan.

I look over to see you watching me attentively. You watch and listen to see what I do next. I put my caressing finger in my wet pussy and I moan. "Fuck yeah". Do you like what you see?" I ask.

You go over to me and you kneel with your head in my crotch. You put your cheek on my pubic hair, take a deep breath and growl. Of course, this makes me much more moist.

"Put your leg over my shoulder and hold on to my head," you tell me. While I follow your instructions, you bury your face in my dripping pussy and lick me like a melting ice cream cone. Your moaning is driving me fucking crazy. Your hot, wet tongue sucking up all the juices my horny body produces.

"Damn it! Holy shit! That feels so good." I yell. "Please don't stop."

Your tongue alternately circles around my clitoris and sweeps into my pussy to catch my juices. My thighs are covered, too. Your tongue is driving me into a fit of insanity. I push my pussy even harder into your face.

"That's it, baby. Fuck you on my tongue, just like you need it." I can hear it between my legs. With your permission, I'm gonna start rocking my hips faster and faster back and forth until I'm ready to come down harder than I ever have before.

You're moving away. "No, no, no, no, no," I keep repeating.

You undo your fly and pull out your stiff dick. Holy shit, that looks good. Without asking, I get down on my knees and throw myself on you. I'll take as much as I can. My head is bobbing like crazy.

You moan your encouragement, "Fuck the baby. Just like that. Take it all, baby." You grab the back of my head and shove your dick down my throat. I choke a little while choking around your long, thick cock. You pull my head away so I can catch my breath before you start fucking my face.

Suddenly you pull me back up. You kiss me hard and pull my leg up to your hips. "Your dick is so close to my dripping pussy Please, God, stick it in and fuck me."

You do it. Your tight cock keeps pounding into me over and over again while you growl sexy dirty talk in my ear. "Is this what you wanted? Uh, huh. Take it all. I'm gonna come so hard in your tight little pussy. Oh, fuck yeah."

With your sexy words ringing out in my head, you pinch my nipples and I break them, screaming, "Fuck yeah! Just like that. So yummy! Motherfucker, YEEEEEEESSSSSSSSS!"

"Here I come, baby. This tight pussy is choking my dick off. I can't hold it anymore." you say before you grunt your release.

Your sperm dripping down my legs. We're both panting and leaning heavily against the wall. You lay me down on the bed. Cover me up and let me get some much-needed rest.

OWNED

So I injected earlier in my election. I got horny and touched myself. Rubbed my nipples. Caressed my clitoris until it was super hard and came Lately the horniness has gotten worse and worse. Worse because I'm no longer able to control it. I want to touch myself? I have to ask. I want to let myself be forgotten? I ask again. To come? Well, that's what I ask.

I ask you for relief after you have repeatedly allowed me to approach you. Will you let me come or send me on my way? I'm not sure. I'm never sure. So I wait. And I beg you. Beg for the chance to please your pussy. Because let's be honest. This is what it is... yours.

I wake up in pain. I wish for relief. But no. Today is just a fringe day. I'm only able to bring myself to the edge. And I do. Over and over again. Until I feel like I'm going crazy. They stop me because I've lost all control over myself. I let the feelings come. I feel the cutting joy. The pleasure that doesn't quite understand me. So close. But not close enough. Then they send me on a mission or force me to lie down in bed.

I toss and turn. Legs spread wide apart. I drag my hard clitoris against the mattress. It feels so fucking good. Think about whether you'd like it if I fucked my mattress. Knowing that I can't touch myself until you say I wake up in the night desperately looking for a message from you Will she tell me I've been good today? Or will she say what a dirty bitch I got so damn close to you just to make you walk away? Away from the pleasure I'm so close to.

So close. Now that the days are getting short, I know what to expect. Knowing that coming is not an option. So I'll play with your pussy. I'll play until I feel the start of an orgasm. The tension in my body. The beginning of the tingling. The tightening of my muscles and the arching of my back. I know that's all I get, so I enjoy it, NO indulging in this nearness. Knowing that I'm going to feel tingly and needy for a while.

I love sending you messages. Letting you know how well I treat your pussy. Letting you know how good I feel. I'm begging you. Even on the days on the edge when there's little or no hope. I think I definitely won't come if I don't ask, but there's at least a teeny chance if I beg really well.

ALL THE LOVE IN THE WORLD BY ROSE REED

Okay. So usually it's hopeless because you made the rules for a reason. I know that. I know what's expected. I know what's allowed. I do my best to make your pussy happy. If it's allowed to caress and rub my clit I get closer and closer to the drop. I fight against my desire to fall.

Could I do it and not tell you? But of course. But where's the fun in that? I like being a good girl for you. To know that I've pleased you by going crazy with lust and stopping. Stopping for you. Just as you please. Because the shame I would feel if I didn't succeed isn't worth the orgasm I would win. Lying through denial would cloud the waters. It's not worth it. The truth always wins.

A sperm night is a little tenser. Even if I jerk off, only with your permission. Does it come easy? Ha! No. Of course not. I have to work for it. Bring your pussy over and over again. Begging you like a good bitch to let your pussy come off.

No? Mild disappointment. Little bit of anger too. After all, it is sperm night. But no. No means no. So I'm stopping. Restraint is about the feelings of a marginalized day. Sometimes I want to hurt you. I get so frustrated; I want to punch you or kick you. Have a fit. But I make a smartass remark and thank you for allowing me to kick myself. Another night of tossing and turning. I know there will be no relief the next day either. It's another day of being on the edge.

But oh yes days. What a wonderful time. As always, I'll take your pussy to the point where she can't bear not to come. I quit. I'll let the feelings fade a bit before I go again. My wand is your pussy's favorite friend. Even vibration on the hard clitoris, which you control. Close. So fucking close that I sweat and shake. I sweat and shake. Please? Oh fuck, please let me cum. Can I please? You take a break. Oh, shit, I'm so close. I can hardly hold it in anymore. I pull the wand away. I'll pause with you to gain some sanity.

More attention to the aching clitoris pulsating between my legs. I just want to feel. To want to feel these wonderful feelings forever. To know that I can't hold on forever. I want to please you. I want your happiness and your approval. Damn, it feels so good. I tell you, I'm back. So close. You're killing me. Denial of my orgasm only makes me feel stronger.

Please? Fuck, please? I want your pussy to come? Can I please? Please tell me yes. Please let me release this tension that's building up in my body? Please let your pussy come? Please let it come. So close. I wanna jerk off. Fuck please?

I beg and I beg. Typing like crazy in my frenzy. I want liberation. I want you inside me. Fuck, fuck, fuck, fuck, fuck. Oh, please? And then, "Yeah, let my pussy get hard." I smile. Knowing that it's time to make you happy. To make your pussy feel as good as it can feel at this moment. Thank you. Even before I come, because I can't forget it in my horny mist. I can't forget to thank the one who controls my pussy and wallows in it The one who encourages me to please myself and my pussy.

Then I climb up the abyss again frantically. Knowing that this time I can fall. I can fall hard. They convey more encouragement. Telling me to get your pussy shot off now, damn it. Just to fucking do it. You send sexy words that bring me closer and closer to you. Goddamn it! Then I'm there. God, I wish you were here to witness what you've made of me. I think about you. I wish you'd do that and I'd break. Mostly I bite my lip to smother the noise. unable to let go of the moaning and screaming, begging to be let out. All the pressure eases and I start to float a little.

I'm jamming up again. Knowing that you're giving multiple orgasms is not just a possibility, it's a fucking necessity. I'm too much at the point where I can't stop. I feel like I have to keep going until my body collapses or I just can't come anymore. And I fucking do. Over and over again. I listen to your voice. Looking at my pictures of you. Sometimes I watch porn I'll share with you someday so you know exactly what I came so hard for. I take breaks to update you on how many sperm I had or how hard they were. Maybe to tell you how wet I am, or to explain the mess I'm making.

Then you tell me to stop.

And I do.

I stop and enjoy the moment, the feelings that you have evoked from my body, excuse your body, because it is all yours now. I let my heavy breathing subside. I relax and enjoy the sexual ecstasy you have evoked. The tingling that wanders from my clitoris through my body. Then I report.

I enjoy the reporting almost as much as the actual buzzing. Because you like me like this. I'll let you know what wonders you're allowed to be. I explain in detail, even though I'm rather embarrassed. Knowing the details makes it real for you too. Knowing that you smile when you read makes it real for you too. I hope you'll stroke the cock that I wish so much to be in front of me. Waiting for my favorite part. When you explain how well I've done and how pleased you are with me. It makes me feel special. Because I could bring you joy, too.

The only thing I like more are your explanations of how you came to me later. What exactly you did and how you felt. How my actions made you want to please yourself. How letting go ultimately kept me in power.

PARASAILING TO PARADISE

When I was on holiday with my best friend, one day we signed up for a parasailing activity. I was a bit scared because I was flying so high, but I'll try it. Karen can be pretty persuasive.

The day of the parasailing, Karen begs to go. I choose myself. I make it to the dock just in time to jump on board, and off I go.

I immediately notice this really sexy man moving around the boat as if he were on land. I noticed this because my clumsy ass was almost planted with his face on the way to my seat in front. He clamps on the first couple and checks that they're comfortable. And off they go.

I look up, along with everyone else. Holy shit! I can do this. I can do this. I need a distraction. Hmmm! Hot chick's heading for the front of the boat. Perfect! Oh, what I would do for that. He looks over and catches me staring. Smooth from my side, I know. I can feel my cheeks starting to burn.

When I look back, he takes off his shirt and throws it in a storage room. I'm ready to melt. Wow! Lots of tanned, muscular skin. I just wanna take his chest from his shoulders to his... Oh, God! I gotta stop this shit. My nipples got hard and I started tingling between my legs. I feel his eyes on my chest. He lifts them up so he can look me in the eyes again. This time with a grin on his bulging lips.

The couple comes down. The boat stops to swap people. Hottie asks if I'm ready.

Fuck yes, I'm ready! Oh, he's talking about putting me in the sky all by myself. He goes to unstrap the last couple while I try to make my way to the back of the boat without making a fool of myself.

When I get to the man who makes me more than normally nervous, I grab my foot at the end of the hippie skirt I just had to wear. Damn it! BAM!!! Right into a hard chest vibrating with his laugh.

Please just shoot me. He's hooking me up. His hands check the strap. I moan as he accidentally touches a nipple as he pulls the seatbelt. The eyes meet again. I almost gasp at this point. He whispers to me, "Where's your friend?"

I'm asking if it's a problem that I don't have anyone with me. He surprises me by jumping up with practiced ease and hooking himself in.

The boat starts to move and we start to climb. Oh shit! I grab my knees in a death grip. My fingers turn white at the tips. Hottie's hand comes to rest on my left hand. Hello!! What's he doing? His hand squeezes mine, and I look down as it gradually slides up my leg.

Holy hell, my chest rises as I struggle to breathe. As his hand reaches my hip, he whispers in my ear and asks if I'm okay. This is all I can do to shake my head. His hand moves to my pussy and starts rubbing. God, that feels so fucking good! I don't want him to stop, so I look at the ocean way below us.

My grip on my knees has relaxed. I move them up to brush my nipples. I circle them slightly and hardly touch them anymore. The pressure between my legs has increased. I feel myself approaching the climax. The ocean around us is beautiful! I feel like I'm going to explode. I squeeze both nipples strongly together and let out a scream that I can only imagine carrying back to the boat.

We are pulled back down again. I have to pull it together. Hottie gets loose and starts working on my straps. He tells me to wait while he fastens the next two.

They go up. Sexy McHotness helps me find my way to the back of the boat. He sits down and pulls me into his lap. I fall on a very hard cock. I wiggle and I hear him gasp.

I feel my skirt lift up at the back as the boat starts to move. The wobbly skirt still covers my lap and legs. A whisper in my ear "lift me up very quickly". I do what he says.

At this point, I'm pretty sure I'm dreaming or losing my mind. When I sit down again, I feel my naked skin against his trunk. His hand dives inches under my skirt and pulls my suit aside. He moans as he finds the moisture he has caused. I look around. What the hell are we doing here?

Everyone's looking up. The boat hits a wave. Hottie's finger gets shoved violently into my wet hole. My God! "Excuse me" is whispered in my ear.

"'S okay' is all I can get out. I can feel him moving again. Holy shit.

One more whisper, "Can you be quiet?" I'm shaking my head, yeah. His finger's leaving me. I moan a little about loss. We hit another wave, and he lifts me up enough to push me on his dick. We sit still while my body adjusts.

When the boat hits several waves, I am lifted and pushed back on his tail. God, yes! I have to stay calm. Fortunately, the engine, the waves and the talk of the people around us help to hide my whimpering and moaning that slips out.

The ocean seems to get choppier and choppier as the boat rises and falls violently. I concentrate on the thick cock that keeps ramming into my dripping pussy over and over again.

Oh shit, I'm about to hum again. My new friend reaches over and pinches my clit between his fingers. I turn around and bite his shoulder and try to muffle my screams. He pushes roughly into me again and empties into me while my pussy strangles his cock in waves.

Awesome! The boat starts to slow down. Mr Rock, my world needs to get back to work. I grin a little because I'm not the only one with wobbly legs now.

SPOONING/MINDFUCK

When it's time to go to sleep, we crawl into bed. It's been a long day. We are both so tired that we have wished for nothing more than to have our heads banging against our pillows. We lie down. Me with my back to you. You push up against me from behind to spoon.

"Goodnight babe," you whisper in my ear.

"Goodnight," I say while closing my eyes.

As I lie there with my eyes closed, the rest of my senses become hypersensitive. At first I think I'll be all right. I listen intently to your breath so close to my ear. I smell the masculine soap from your shower. I feel your arm around my waist and your legs tucked into mine. Your chest rises and falls calmly against my back.

Then it happens. I notice your cock half-hard against my ass. I'm at the end. My mind makes me remember exactly how good I can feel with your cock. I slide back to press harder against you.

"Shut up", you growl in my ear. Which makes it even worse. I love how your voice always gets all deep and growling when we play. Fuck. I don't have to move.

Where just a few moments ago I was so tired that I could have fallen asleep on my feet, now I'm full of butterflies and dirty thoughts. My brain is spinning as I try not to move an inch. I know you're tired. We both worked so hard today. A busy day all around.

I can't stop my mind. He's pushing me to take you in hand. To caress my favorite cock until you enter me. Fuck, no! Stop thinking that shit! Go to sleep.

I'm trying to slow my breathing down. I'm trying to relax my body. How the fuck can you lie so still? Why is your breathing so calm? I'm going crazy!

Was that a twitch? Did your dick move? I catch myself wiggling my ass a little. Fuck, fuck, fuck! I didn't mean to move. I want you to get your sleep. But I also want you to turn on your back and suck that beautiful cock until you get your hands in my hair and put it in my mouth. Fill my mouth until you're hard enough to put me on it. Riding it until we're both too tired to ever move again.

Damn woman! Get a hold of yourself! I can't show my face when I'm not tired. If I lie here long enough, I'm sure I'll doze off. Isn't that right?

You're still very calm. Your breathing pattern doesn't seem to have changed. My breathing has become much faster.

Your arm is moving and your hand is resting on my chest. ARE YOU FUCKING KIDDING ME?! As I breathe, your fingertips brush against my nipple. FUCK! I feel them burst open. My breathing is getting faster. . I squeeze my legs. I'm trying to get some kind of relief. Nothing but your cock will help me.

The laundry. Think of tons of laundry that needs to be washed, dried, folded and put away. Dirty laundry. Dirty sheets. Mmmmmm. How I'd love to get those sheets dirty. I'd like you to rub me while you hold me. I want to cum for you and watch your sperm shoot out of your amazing cock.

I'm squirming again. Your cock is rubbing against my ass. That reminds me how wonderful that cock in my ass would feel. Your fingers are stroking my nipple again. It's tingling from my nipple to my pussy. I'm squirming again. I crunch lightly on this wonderful cock.

I try to lie still. Damn it! I told you what happens to me when I lie like this. Then I feel your fingers snapping and twisting on my sensitive nipple. I hear your faint giggle in my ear. "You lasted almost 15 minutes, babe. I am so proud of you. You know I told you to ask for whatever you want. No need to torture yourself when I'm here, ready to fuck that sweet body until you're really ready to sleep. All you have to do is ask," you remind me.

"Please take care of me. I'm losing my mind. I've tried so hard to settle down. I just need you. I just need you. Please." I'm begging you.

You slide your other arm under me and pinch and twist both nipples while you rub your hardened cock against my ass. I reach back and grab your ass. I can feel the muscles tightening and relaxing. Shit! I'm pumping my hips back into yours because I want more.

One hand slowly slides down my stomach and splits my pussy lips. The fingers slide down. They're giggling again. "Babe, you're so wet. You're so wet. Mmmm!" Your fingers give me a second to find your mouth. You growl in my ear while you suck my juices off your fingers. I arch my back and hold your ass.

"Please. I'm ready." I push. You straighten your hard cock up and it slides right into my pussy. So warm and wet. My stupid mind has taken care of foreplay tonight. Now I just hold on for the main event.

*Well normally I wouldn't end up with a cliffhanger like this BUT my emphasis is on what a mind fuck can do by just spooning it out.

SURPRISE

They tell me how beautiful my nipples are. I grin from ear to ear and I'm so proud that you like my body. Just being around you makes them perk up. Hard nipples stick out. Now that I know you enjoy them so much, I don't worry about padded bras. They make me wear little or no lacy bras, so it's obvious when I think of you.

Today you come to visit with a small package. Oh dear! A surprise! I love surprises! It hardly matters what it is. The thought that you thought you would please me and win another smile is the real plus for me. I jump up and down in my excitement. You hug me tightly and turn me around before you put my feet back on the ground.

Your smile tells me that you are satisfied with my reaction. Which gives me even more pleasure. "Go ahead and open it, Baby Girl", you push.

My hands shake a little when I unpack and look at what's in my hands. My cheeks turn bright red as I giggle and dig into your chest. You give me a great big hug before we talk any further.

"I love her! Thank you so much! I "m so excited to see how they feel! I hope you'll like them!" I wander around in my excitement.

They lift my shirt over my head, fold it and put it on the table. I stand completely still while you pinch both nipples and kneel down to take them in your mouth one by one. Your hot, wet mouth always feels so good. When I lick and suck thoroughly, I squirm in the blink of an eye.

You get up and take back my gift. You open the clamp, slide it onto a nipple and pull it tight until I squirm a little bit. "Are you okay, little girl?" you ask.

I nod my head. "Yes. Thank you," I giggle. I'm so excited about my new ouchie and the attention you give my nipples.

You go ahead and attach the second one. You pinch and twist my nipple, just the way I love it. Again you tighten it and you look at me because I nod. I bounce around a little to see the chain move and my titty wiggles. I giggle and whimper a little while I pick up the things I feel.

If you take a step back, stare at my newly adored nipples. They pinch just enough to give me my happy ouchies. There is a chain between each clip. I love chains so much. They tighten the clamps until I just whimper a little. "My sweet girl looks so sexy right now."

I blush with pride and stand even higher and push my breast out for you. The pain is so sweet. It tingles from my nipples down to my pussy, which is definitely moist for you. You pull the chain so I can follow you into the kitchen.

You sit down at the kitchen table, and I go to make you a glass of ice water and a snack. With every move, my jewellery tugs at my nipples and makes that beautiful sound chains make. I squeeze my legs together and try so hard to concentrate on my task.

Water, cheese, fruit. Water, cheese, fruit. Water, cheese, fruit. I repeat it in my head so I don't get distracted. At this point, I get a little nervous. I'm all excited with my ouchies and I know you're watching me closely.

I put the plate and the glass on the table and put them in front of you. You lift the chain up to my mouth. "Don't you dare let go," you ask. I take the chain between my teeth and smile at the pain in my nipples. The chain now scoffs and pulls at my nipples.

You eat your snack leisurely and sip your water. Occasionally you reach over to bang my ass or rub my pussy just to torture me. I grind my teeth in the chain and do my best not to let go.

After you're done, you take me to the bathroom and bend me over the sink. You unzip your pants and take your hard cock in your hand. I smile when I see how turned on you are. You line up my favourite cock in a row. It's barely in my pussy anymore.

When you turn around, you look into my eyes in the mirror. Your hands go to the clamps on my nipples. As you quickly open the clamps, you punch inside me. The intense fucking pain in my nipples makes me scream through my clenched teeth and my body cramps around your wonderful cock. My pain and lust induced orgasm rocks me.

Nearby you rub my clitoris and fuck me fast and hard. It builds up until I cum again, only to squeeze an orgasm out of you too. Boy, do I love my new jewelry.

CUCK TO COCK

For the first time I was possessed by cuckold, after I had been royally betrayed by my then wife. I had a vague idea of what was happening at that time, but nothing that even remotely corresponded to the reality I was to experience at close quarters.

One afternoon, when I was supposedly away on business, I returned home in the afternoon and hid in a storage cupboard overlooking our bedroom. Yes, I was suspicious. And in fact, she was not alone when she came home from work.

They started having drinks in the living room. At that point, I couldn't see either of them, but I could hear them clearly. They didn't waste much time either; the conversation quickly turned to how much they wanted to fuck each other. Soon I heard heavy breathing and passionate kissing sounds. Whatever he did to her, she was extremely responsive. "Yes," she kept saying. "Yes, yes, more, more, more, more!" Then I heard clapping sounds, soft at first, then harder. He hit her repeatedly. She began to whimper. I was frozen in place, caught between the humiliation and the intense sexual heat.

When they appeared in the bedroom and I could see her from my hiding place, she was naked while he still had his pants on. I had to admit he was a good-looking guy. She was as beautiful as ever.

She started begging him to hit her before she fucked him. I knew about her masochistic streak, of course, but she hadn't asked me for it for a long, long time. I was humiliated. He pulled a heavy leather belt out of his jeans and immediately she went ass up and face down on the bed. I could not believe my eyes! Where did that come from? I didn't dare move a muscle or say a word as he put the belt up her ass and thighs. He had dyed her bright red and began to raise welts and purple bruises before finally stopping. She seemed ecstatic.

Next he started to fuck her throat deep, started beating on her pussy, then he rammed his cock balls deep into her ass, all in quick succession. Then he reversed the order: ass, cunt, throat, then back and forth indiscriminately, stopping to give her another beating, this time on her tits. At this point she screamed and grunted, screamed obscenities and still demanded more, until finally they hummed and buzzed uncontrollably for several agonizingly long minutes. It was unbearable. It felt like an eternity. I was horrified and bound.

My own cock was painfully hard, but my attention was commanded by the sight and sound of his magnificent cock plowing her ass. He pulled it all the way out and then pushed it back in until it reached the handle, each time causing a throaty growl deep down her throat. Again and again and again and again. His shaft was huge, uncut and rock hard, extra long and thick, furiously stained red and purple, bent straight up, with a huge mushroom head and a massive pair of balls hanging low and heavy, obviously brimming with his sperm. He had incredible stamina.

I was fascinated by myself. Where had she found him? How long had she been fucking him? I was speechless. I couldn't shape the thoughts in my brain to express how angry and humiliated I felt. And I couldn't even begin to admit to myself how much I wanted to feel that cock inside me.

He pulled himself out of it one last time and started to move towards the front of the bed again, when he suddenly looked up and seemed to close his eyes with me, right where I was sure I was safely hidden from view. No! He could not actually see me! But he just kept staring, as if he was looking right through me, without any recognizable expression. Or was that just the faintest glimmer of amusement?

Finally he turned his attention back to her, kissed her deeply and put her fingers around his swollen shaft, took her hand in his and moved towards her face. Then she lifted him up energetically and screamed dirty and loving things until finally he roared and sprayed an ungodly amount of thick white cum onto her hair, face, eyes, nose and of course into her wide open mouth and outstretched tongue. He warned her not to swallow a drop.

Of course he came and caught me in my hiding place. Of course he ordered me to eat his sperm off her face, every single drop, before kissing her deeply and drinking the rest down. And of course I followed eagerly.

That afternoon I landed on my knees as he shot another load into my neck, then on all fours as he put a third in my ass, which he now called my pussy. Finally, as he was getting ready to say goodbye, he kissed her passionately one last time, held her firmly in his arms and said, "I told you this was how it was going to end.